All I Need

The once spoiled and selfish Bri Cleyvon, ignored her parents and married Tyrone Grant against their wishes. Now disowned by her wealthy and influential family, Bri realized her costly mistake too late. Now, with her infant son in her arms, she flees her abusive husband like the hounds-of-hell are nipping at her heals. And when word of her father's illness reaches her, Bri knows in her heart of heart that it's time to face her parents and beg for their forgiveness.
When Trevet located Bri, he held fast in his dislike for her. He remembered how spoiled, disrespectful, and selfish she was, not caring one iota about the affects her actions were having on her parents. If he had his way, he would leave her "little butt" in Virginia. But, that was not his call. The craziest thing was after reconnecting with this new and improved Bri, he knew he was in trouble. She was not only beautiful, kind, and intelligent but an incredible mother. What more could any man ask for, but the devil on his shoulder kept taunting, "are you ready for this incredible woman and this thing called love?"

Dedication

Lena H. My Collaborator My Sister, My Friend, My Muse

Acknowledgements

Lee Summers Editor
Cover Design

Renee Luke Cover Me – Book Covers

Chapter One

Darkness loomed before her as she sped up the dark, deserted road. The only fact known to Bri Cleyvon-Grant was she had to get out of the small backwoods town as quickly as possible. She didn't know where she was going, but she just had to get out of the state of New Jersey. She glanced in the rearview mirror. A smile touched her lips as she looked at the reflection of the sleeping infant in the car seat behind her. In her heart, she knew she had done the right thing by running from her worthless husband, Tyrone Grant. She should have done it a long time ago. Remorseful tears filled her eyes. No, she chided herself, don't you dare cry. You chose this life. You ignored all the warning signs about Tyrone. How many times did her mother tell her he was wrong for her? She shook her head in rueful disbelief. Why is it women think we can change a sorry man? However, no more, she vowed - no more. Tears filled her eyes anyway, falling in large drops to her lap.

"Why are you crying? You did this to yourself," she said aloud, swiping the tears angrily from her bruised face. She glanced briefly at the time on the car radio: it read two thirty in the morning. She sighed with relief when she saw the streetlights illuminating up ahead. The narrow, desolate road widened into a quiet highway, and she couldn't miss the large lit sign on the side of the road reading "City of Vineland."

Hopefully, she'd find a motel for the night. Welcoming streetlights and traffic lights shone in the car as she slowed to a stop at the end of each block in the quaint small town. Bri glanced at her baby, thankful he was still asleep. She exhaled a relieved breath when she pulled into Days Inn's motel parking lot. Turning off the car, she grabbed her purse and moved to the back, gently lifting the baby from the back seat before entering the building.

"Can I help you?" the friendly desk clerk asked and smiled. She took a moment to take in her surroundings. The motel was luxurious compared to some of the seedy places she had stayed with Tyrone.

"Yes, I'd like a room for a couple of nights, please," she said, sitting the baby carrier on the counter. "King or Double?"

"King, please."

"Fill out the registration card, and I will need some ID," the clerk instructed.

Bri nodded, reached into her purse then handed the clerk her Georgia license. She quickly filled out the registration card.

"How old is the beautiful baby?" the clerk inquired politely. She looked over at her son.

"Thanks. He's a month old," she answered, smiling. She handed him the card, along with her credit card.

The one smart thing Bri did was she never told Tyrone about the trust that came into effect when she turned twenty-one, six months ago. The only decent thing that came of her relationship with Tyrone was her son, Aaron.

"Okay, Ms. Cleyvon, Room 116. Do you need any help with anything?" the clerk asked.

"If you could help with my bags in the car, I would appreciate it." The clerk came from behind the desk to aid her. Thankful for his help, she gave him a generous tip.

"Miss?" the clerk said, standing outside her hotel room door with concern on his face. "I don't mean to pry, but are you okay?" Bri understood why he asked. He couldn't miss the many bruises and swollen areas on her face resulting from Tyrone's last beating. Bri smiled at the man.

"Yes, I am now. Thank you for your concern." "Okay, miss. If you need anything, just call the front desk and ask for Henry."

"Thank you, Henry, I will." Bri closed the door and leaned against it, sighing with relief. She was finally free and felt it. She doubted Tyrone would come after her; at least, she prayed he wouldn't. She's so finished with Tyrone and his dysfunctional life. And to think she had given up her family for him. Many times, she had asked herself what was it about Tyrone that would cause her to turn her back on her family. Bri Cleyvon was born in Atlanta, Georgia, to Jorge Aaron Cleyvon and Irene Cleyvon, prominent attorneys in Greater Atlanta and surrounding areas and was of the wealthiest African American families in Georgia. Being the only child, her parents doted on her and thoroughly spoiled her. Bri wanted the best and accepted nothing less. That was until she went off to college and met Tyrone Grant, an employee at the Morris Brown College cafeteria where she attended. Her standards then went out the window. Bri was thoroughly infatuated with the beautiful, coffee-colored man. Even though he was not an overly tall man, he had a fantastic body and knew it. He was clean-shaven with a squared jaw line, full lips beneath a straight nose, and gorgeous deep brown eyes. She was not the only co-ed who wanted him. He captured many of the young girls' hearts that attended the university. He was beautiful, and when he smiled at her, she fell madly in love with him. They started dating, and Tyrone was flattering, extremely attentive and always behaved like a gentleman. She wanted the relationship to advance and tried many times to seduce him, but Tyrone would stop her, saying he wanted to wait until they were married. She was in love. It turned out to be the worst day of her life when she took Tyrone home to meet her parents. Her parents were coolly cordial. Her father gave Tyrone the third degree about his future; her mother all but told him she didn't like him for her daughter. When they finally left her home and parents, Tyrone was incensed. That was the night she lost her virginity. He had taken her brutally, and after it was over, she cried for hours. That was the side of Tyrone she ignored, that violent, angry side of him. She never thought it was supposed to be like that, not with the man you loved; and the sex didn't get any better. After that, all he cared about was how much money her parents had. She loved Tyrone, or at least she thought she did. When she refused to do some of the wild things that frightened her, he would call her stuck up, start accusing her of being a snob like her parents, or state she thought she was better than he was. Of course, she did all she could do to persuade him otherwise. When her parents wouldn't bend on their opinion of Tyrone, she ignored their worries and anxiety. If she started voicing her doubts about their relationship, he would turn into the man she first met.

Later, Tyrone convinced her to marry him. When she announced her nuptials to her parents, they had the biggest argument she had ever had in her life, going as far as threatening to disown her, but she was in love. After dropping out of school, Bri followed her husband anywhere he wanted to go. They never stayed in one town long enough to set down any roots. They constantly moved from one town to the next. Each place they moved to; Tyrone seemed to attract the rough elements of that city. It was not above her to work at a fast food restaurant just to have money in their pockets. Tyrone always seemed unable to find a job but never failed to use what little money they had to waste on booze and drugs. When she told Tyrone she was pregnant, he became furious and demanded she get an abortion because he didn't want or like kids. Fortunately for her, they didn't have the kind of money it took to pay for an abortion, and from that time on, he never failed to tell her what a disappointment she was to him. She recalled the night he came back to the motel where they lived, uptight and frantic. He literally dragged her out of the bed and forced her to leave with him. Later, she found out he had stolen some weed from one of his degenerate associates. That's how they ended up in New Jersey.

Bri was eight months pregnant, and after they lived in the car for a few days, Tyrone befriended some brothers at a bar. After telling them his hard luck story, they let them move into their small apartment; who lived practically in squalor with his so-called friends. All they did was drink and abuse drugs while she worked at any odd job she could obtain. Tyrone took the money she made, and he, along with his derelict friends, partied until there was no money left. The one time she asked him why he didn't get a job, he became insanely outraged. That was the first time he beat her, screaming all the while how much he hated her and her stuck up type. He accused her of trapping him by becoming pregnant.

"If you hate me so much, why do you keep me around? Just let me go," she screamed at him.

"Because I know you have money somewhere," he always reminded her.

"You forget my parents disowned me because of you," she would remind him, and for that, she was beaten.

What Tyrone didn't know was she had a half a million-dollar trust fund that her parents had no control over, left to her by her grandmother. Bri knew if he had any knowledge about the money she would never get away from him. When she went into labor, one of his bum friends dropped her off at the hospital emergency room. Tyrone didn't bother to come to the hospital. Her son's birth certificate read Jorge Aaron Cleyvon... No father listed. Having no money and nowhere to go, she returned to the apartment and Tyrone. She had to do something; he had started insisting she get a job now that she'd given birth. There was no way she was leaving her baby with him and his friends. Again, she was beaten one day because the baby was taking too much of her attention from him. His drinking and drugging were taking its toll, and he was now an outright drug addict. He did anything to get his next fix. She knew she had to get away before he killed her. Bri also realized if he beat her, eventually he would turn his anger on her son. She would kill him first before she let him put a hand on her baby. The day she turned twenty-one, which Tyrone knew nothing about or cared, she started preparing for her escape every day with the ruse she was going job hunting and taking the baby to the sitter. She contacted her bank in Atlanta and started the proceedings to release her trust fund and make her funds available to her. In her heart, she knew she didn't deserve the Trust; she had been a horrible daughter. Her plan was to use only what was needed for her and the baby to relocate and settle. Then she would devote her time to her art to make a living. She began secretly buying and packing things she needed for the baby and herself, storing them in the trunk of the car. When she had all she needed, she waited for her opportunity. After the last beating and Tyrone fell into his drug-induced stupor, she bundled up her baby and left Tyrone passed out in the backwoods of New Jersey.

Looking at her reflection in the mirror, she gingerly touched the swollen eyes, split lips, and cut chin. Tyrone had beaten her before but never like this. He was always selective as to where his punches would land. It was always her body - never her face. She guessed now it didn't matter where his fists landed. Three years had taken its toll on her. Turning away disgusted, she gazed at her beautiful, slumbering infant. Aaron was starting to stir, and the heaviness of her breasts indicated her son needed feeding. As Aaron nursed, she thought about where they would go. Sadly, Bri realized right away that she could never go back to Atlanta. She was too ashamed to face her parents now. Virginia, she thought… Virginia Beach. She always loved it there.

"Well, little fellow, Virginia Beach will soon be our new home."

Chapter Two

Two years later

Trevet Harrison strolled leisurely through the small, intimately-lit art gallery. He had been asked to locate the daughter of Jorge Cleyvon, by the man himself. There was no favor too large for him to do for Jorge Cleyvon. If he wanted his daughter found, found is what she shall be. After a year plus of searching, he finally obtained information on the whereabouts of Bri Cleyvon. His break came when he noticed activity on her trust fund, from which she withdrew a large amount of money that gave him all her information and her whereabouts. What puzzled him is why she had not withdrawn from the trust fund since she turned twenty-one. He cringed when unpleasant memories filled his head at the thought of seeing Bri Cleyvon again.

She was about eighteen years old when he first started working for her father's law firm. More times than not, she would burst into her father's office like a hurricane, demanding from her father one thing or another. Bri was a beautiful, self-centered, and spoiled young woman. He didn't like her then and was sure she was probably the same selfish, spoiled brat he remembered. He recalled how distraught Jorge was when she married Tyrone Grant against his wishes. In anger, he threatened to disown her. However, the threat didn't faze her; she wanted Tyrone, and that was all that mattered to her. Unknown to Bri, Jorge never went forward with the threat. She left with Grant, and her parents had not heard from her in three years. Trevet didn't know what to expect from Jorge's daughter, but he would take her home kicking and screaming if he had to.

Trevet observed the multitude of art lovers and dealers strolling around the room. They scrutinized and commented on the exhibition of paintings that lined the wall of the gallery. He moved slowly around the patrons until a painting caught his eyes. Stopping, he gazed at the face of a young black woman. Her face was tilted downward with a white mask painted on her face; her eyes were closed. One hand was on the side of her face as if to hold the mask in place. The unique thing about the portrait was the white mask was crumbling away, but what captivated him most was the sadness on the face as the mask crumbled. The image touched him.

"What do you think?" a feminine voice beside him said.

Trevet looked over at the elegantly dressed older woman beside him. "Intriguing," he replied honestly. "Yes," she agreed. "Makes me wonder if she is sad or relieved."

Trevet nodded. "Do you know the artist?"

"Oh yes, Bri Cleyvon; pleasant young woman."

"Pleasant?" Trevet repeated, his interest piqued.

"Oh yes, this is her exhibit. She's a lovely girl… very reserved and extremely private." Trevet frowned. That person wasn't the Bri Cleyvon he knew.

"Has she any family?" he asked. The woman shrugged.

"Never mentioned any, but she has an adorable little boy." Trevet gave a silent grunt. So Bri had Tyrone Grant's child.

The woman looked up at the exceptionally tall, handsome man beside her. Immediately, she could see he was in excellent physical condition by the way his shirt molded to his broad shoulders and tapered down to the waistband of his belted slacks. Slightly flustered by her wayward thoughts, her eyes surveyed him. He was a handsome man, she thought – no, a beautiful man: cinnamon colored complexion with dark short hair that was neatly trimmed, gray eyes and a tapered nose. His mouth held her gaze; perfection was her thought. He possessed a fine mouth that could have been sculpted, along with a strong jaw line and small dimpled chin. To be young again, the woman thought with a silent chuckle.

"Would you care to meet her?" the woman said and smiled warmly. Trevet nodded. She looked around the room.

"There," she pointed in Bri's direction. "She's pretty, yes," the woman said, smiling.

Trevet looked in the direction the woman indicated. Pretty was an understatement. She was perfect. She appeared to be listening intently to an invited patron of the showing. A slight smile was on her full, shapely mouth that he noticed didn't quite reach her almond-shaped, brown eyes. His gaze traveled over her. The light reflected off her reddish brown, shoulder-length hair, which was parted down the middle and loosely brushed her shoulders. The well-lit room accentuated the radiance of her golden honey skin color. She was dressed conservatively in a black cocktail dress with a wide belt, emphasizing her petite waist. The dress flared around her hips and stopped just above her knees to display beautifully shaped legs. Bri Cleyvon was small, standing five feet two inches without the strapped black sandals on her small feet. The photo in his possession did her no justice. Bri was more than just pretty, Trevet surmised. His brow furrowed. There was something different about her; a difference he couldn't quite identify, but whatever it was, it suited her well.

"Come, I'll introduce you," the woman said. Trevet followed the woman to where Bri stood. He stood quietly observing all the changes in Bri while she listened attentively to the older gentleman that held her attention.

"Excuse me, Bri," the older woman interrupted. "This gentleman was admiring your paintings and wanted to meet you," the silver haired woman said and indicated Trevet.

"Hello, Bri," Trevet greeted, observing her reaction. He took in the way her dark eyes widened in surprise then relaxed into what he thought was recognition. Bri looked over at Trevet and instant recognition registered in her eyes. She quickly lowered her head to cover her reaction. When they lifted, the expression was gone. "Hello." She said it so softly, he had to lean in to hear her.

The woman beside him was quite interested in the distant exchange she had just witnessed. "Ms. Dobbs," Bri said softly, "will you excuse us, please?"

Ms. Dobbs nodded and watched as Bri led the handsome man away. Trevet followed; his gaze fell to the gentle sway of her hips as she led him to a small room that appeared to be a sort of storage area. Once behind the closed door, Bri turned to face him. Her eyes met his, rendering him speechless. She was stunning. No woman had ever staggered him. He cleared his suddenly dry throat.

"You remember me?" Trevet asked.

"Yes, you're one of my father's attorneys," she answered quietly. He acknowledged with a nod. "Are my mother and father well?" she asked with concern in her tone.

"Do you really care?" he asked with an arrogant lift of his brow. Bri reacted as if slapped. Her eyes narrowed.

"Yes, I do, contrary to what you may believe or have heard about my parents' and my situation."

"Does it really matter what I think, Bri?" She looked up at him but did not respond.

"Are they well?" she repeated.

"No, your father is ill, which brings me to why I'm here. He wants me to bring you home," he stated. She turned from him, not wanting to display weakness in front of this cynical man. "I will go with you," she stated simply. "I have only a few minutes left before the exhibit ends. Here is my address." She jotted it down on the back of a card she pulled from the pocket of her dress and handed it to him.

"I need to go home and get my son first," she informed him.

"Do you mind if I stay until the exhibit is over and follow you home?"

"Fine." She turned and left him standing alone.

An hour later, they arrived at her condominium. After paying the babysitter, Bri began packing clothes for herself and the baby. Trevet sat waiting in her spacious, tastefully decorated living room. She had excellent taste, he thought, taking in his surroundings and the way the colors complimented the room. He glanced at his watch, 11:30 pm. He was tired from the drive to Virginia, and it would be a long drive back to Atlanta. Maybe they should wait until morning and leave. This was not a trip he was looking forward to, plus Bri looked exhausted. He'd stayed and watched her move throughout the gallery. He admired the demure way she talked to the interested buyers until the last patron left. No one had to tell him her exhibit was a complete success. He could tell by the many bare spaces on the walls and empty display stands that she'd sold most of her work. As well, he'd heard her being commissioned to do more pieces, to the gallery's delight. He had to admit she was an extraordinarily talented artist; another fact he never knew about her.

Bri returned to the living room. "We'll be ready in a minute. I only have to wake Aaron and then…" she spoke softly.

"I think we should leave in the morning," Trevet offered, feeling guilty that he had pushed her into leaving tonight. "I can't let you awaken the baby; morning is soon enough."

"Thank you," she said quietly relieved. "Have you eaten?" she asked softly. "Can I get you something? I have some leftover fried chicken and potato salad," she offered, avoiding eye contact as she spoke to him.

Trevet wished she would look at him. "Thank you. That would be great."

This was not the Bri Cleyvon he remembered, he thought. She had changed into a shirt and jeans, and her hair was pulled back in a ponytail. She motioned for him to follow. He took a seat at the small table in the kitchen. She opened the fridge and took out a container of fried chicken and potato salad, uncovered them and placed the bowls on the table. Turning to the cabinet, she took out two plate sets and put them on the table, taking a seat across from him.

"Help yourself." Trevet served himself, filling his plate, while Bri took a small amount of food for herself.

Quietly she ate, determined to ignore the handsome, intimidating man across from her. She was still trying to compose her reaction after initially seeing Trevet Harrison at the gallery. She looked up to find his eyes on her.

"How do you remember me?" Trevet broke the silence.

Bri averted her eyes before answering. "I was about eighteen, I guess, when you started working with my father. I used to come to my dad's office a lot. You just didn't notice me," she shrugged.

"I remembered you. You're about what, twenty-four now?" Trevet couldn't help but see the sadness in her eyes when she finally looked at him. Bri glanced up at him. He was still as handsome as she remembered. A little older and more serious looking, but to her he was always serious. The looks he used to give her when she barged into her father's office made her think he would like to beat her spoiled butt. She sighed. That was long ago, and she is nothing like that rambunctious, disrespectful teenager anymore. She turned her attention back to her plate.

"How old is your son?"

"He's twenty months now," she answered. Brie knew by his expression that he was not satisfied with one-word answers. She needed to clear the air with him before they made the trip back to Georgia, if only to make him see she was not the same person that had put her parents through hell.

"Mr. Harrison," she said, "I know you're wondering what happened between me and my parents. Despite all, I love them very much. I know I was a spoiled brat when I left them. I thought I was in love. To me the sun rose and set around Tyrone Grant, but I was wrong. I found out later he was everything my parents said and worse.

Trevet listened intently. "Why didn't you just come home?" he asked.

"They disowned me. I couldn't go back; I was too ashamed," she admitted.

"Not ashamed enough to use their money," Trevet stated sardonically. Her head snapped up, and anger flashed in her eyes.

"Mr. Harrison, first of all, that trust was from my grandmother, and no one knows better than I that I don't deserve it. I only used the trust the one time, and that was to take my son, make a home for him, and escape Tyrone. I had to get away, and when the opportunity presented itself, I slipped away from him in the middle of the night. I had to keep my son safe from him. I was not about to allow him to beat…" she stopped.

"I drove away as fast as possible. We lived in motels for a year, for fear he would come looking for us. I purchased this condo, so I could make a life for my son and concentrate on my art. I have almost repaid the trust, Mr. Harrison, so don't judge me for what I had to do to save the life of me and my child. If Tyrone knew about the trust, I would still be under his control. I know how naïve and stupid I was. I don't need you or anyone to remind me just how foolish I've been and how deeply I hurt my parents. I live with it every day." She stood, took the plates from the table, and placed them in the sink.

Trevet was amazed. Even with her apparent anger and the tears he couldn't miss that filled her eyes while she quietly berated him, she was stunning.

"You knew a lot of people in Atlanta that might have helped you. Why stay so far from home?" he asked. Trevet wanted to back off, but right now, he needed answers. Before he took her back home, he had to make sure this wasn't going to hurt the two people who meant so much to him. It wasn't hard to figure out that she'd suffered at the hands of Tyrone Grant.

"Why, you ask? I know my parents are ashamed of me; I'm ashamed of myself. Why go back to my parents' friends and associates, who no doubt gossiped behind their backs. Their so-called friends that would turn their uppity noses up at me and my son," she paused. "I know, because I was one of them. I hurt my parents deeply; I know that. So rather than go home, I just stayed away to save them the heartache of country club speculation and ridicule."

"So why are you coming now?"

"I love my parents and need to bridge the gap between us. You're coming here made me see it was time, and I would like them to know their grandson. Don't worry, Mr. Harrison, I won't be staying. I'm going to return to Virginia," she said with tears in her voice.

Trevet stepped behind her and touched her softly on the shoulder. She moved away as if scalded, shocked fear on her face. Her reaction to his touch stunned him. Did she think he would hurt her? What happened to Bri Cleyvon, the rambunctious, spoiled young girl? Moving further away from him, she went to the doorway of the kitchen and stopped.

"I have a spare room and bath; everything you need is there. It's up the stairs on your right. Goodnight, Mr. Harrison," she said without looking at him.

Chapter Three

Trevet awoke to the most incredible scent of fresh coffee and wonderful aromas coming from downstairs. The smells assaulted his senses. He glanced at his watch and rose from the bed. It was early. After taking a shower, he dressed quickly. His stomach growled loudly, agreeing that whatever was cooking sure smelled delicious. He couldn't remember the last time he had a home cooked breakfast.

Trevet joined them downstairs. He could hear Bri singing "the alphabet song" while her son sang along in his child's babble; the "Itsy-Bitsy Spider" was the next tune. He gently pushed open the door and watched them. Bri sat in a chair beside her son's highchair. His heart swelled as he witnessed the love and devotion she had for her son. He wanted that kind of love and affection for himself one day. The Cleyvon family was like the family he never had; at least, he always thought of her parents as his family, and they treated him as such.

Having been shuttled from one foster care home to another until the age of eighteen, he hadn't know what it meant to have a mother or father; however, the Cleyvon's turned out to be terrific substitutes. He recalled their meeting. Not knowing his biological parents, he had decided early on that he would never have a family. At age eighteen and out of the system, he had gotten into trouble. That was how he met Mrs. Irene Cleyvon. She was his public defender. He hadn't done anything. Yet, by just hanging around with the wrong crowd, he had been found just as guilty. Mrs. Cleyvon got him off with probation only because this was his first offense.

If it weren't for them, he didn't know where he would have ended up. The Cleyvon's didn't give up on him. They gave him a roof over his head and a job, so he could learn responsibility; then they financed his education and made him part of their family. He remembered the young Bri as a spoiled little girl, whom he avoided at all costs. He used to get so angry with her for not realizing how good she had it. She took everything for granted, and he wanted to spank her little ass for the disrespect she showed her parents. For all these reasons, any request from the Cleyvon's, he granted with no questions asked. She may have appeared to change, but he was not convinced that she had. In the meantime, he would stay close to her parents to make sure she behaved. His focus moved back to mother and son. Bri looked up, and the joy he briefly witnessed on her face disappeared at the sight of him standing in the doorway.

"Good Morning, Mr. Harrison. Please sit and have breakfast," she invited.

Trevet sat in a chair across from the baby, who had quieted when Trevet entered the room. The child was now staring at him. He noticed on the table were ham, grits, eggs, toast, and orange juice. His stomach gave a pleased grumble. Bri's eyes widened when she heard the sound. "Hungry?"

"Famished," he replied sheepishly. "

"Go ahead, Mr. Harrison, help yourself," Bri offered, turning her attention to her son.

Aaron was a handsome boy who favored his mother in looks. He had her same golden honey coloring and dark eyes. She had a plate for herself and a smaller one for the baby with ham cut up in small pieces, eggs, and grits. It sat in front of him. She put his little hands together and blessed the food. At the end, Aaron babbled Amen. Pleased, his mother smiled and gave him his spoon. Aaron began to eat but couldn't seem to get much in his mouth. That's when his mother helped. Trevet watched them. He thought if the boy stopped staring at him, he would possibly take in more food.

"Why don't you just feed him?" Trevet asked logically.

"Because he wants to do it by himself, and I want him to learn independence. He thinks he's doing this himself," she answered, not looking at him.

Trevet dug into his breakfast, occasionally glancing over to see Bri smiling at her son with that undeniable mother's love. There was no mistaking the love for her son. Did she still love the father, he wondered? "Have you heard from your husband?" Trevet asked her.

"No," she said quietly and didn't elaborate. "What about his son?"

"Tyrone has no son," she replied curtly. She wiped the child's face and hands then lifted him from the highchair. "I'm going to clean him up, and then we'll be ready to go," she said, going to the door.

"Bri?" She turned. "Thanks for breakfast."

She nodded and left the room. After everything was packed and the condominium secured, Trevet loaded them in the car while Aaron happily chattered. He slid behind the wheel of a luxury SUV and looked over at Bri before starting the car.

"Why does he look at me so much?" Trevet asked.

"He doesn't know you. Why? Does it bother you?"

"No," he replied and started the car.

The trip to Georgia will be about a ten-hour drive and probably a tedious one, he thought, then glanced over at Bri; she was looking out of the window.

"If you get tired, I'll drive for a while," she offered, not looking at him.

"Thanks."

Aaron fell asleep before they pulled onto the Interstate, and Bri remained silent. She pulled her sketch pad from her tote bag and began doodling. All the company he had was the radio. About noon, Trevet pulled into a diner for lunch, feeling the need to stretch his legs. Trevet stood beside Bri as she lifted Aaron out of the car seat and held him close while Trevet closed the door to the car. Aaron reached for Trevet. He frowned. Bri looked at Trevet, and he did not mistake the challenge in her eyes *let's see what he is going to do.* Trevet accepted the challenge in her eyes and took the baby. She raised her delicate brows in surprise. Satisfied, Aaron looked at his mother with a smile as his arms went around Trevet's neck. Bri smiled back.

At first, Trevet felt uncomfortable. He had never held a baby before but then the child laid his head on his shoulder, and the tension left him. They entered the diner, were shown to a table, and waited while the server brought a highchair for the baby. Trevet leaned close to Bri and attempted to hand Aaron over. His little arms tightened around Trevet's neck.

"Aaron," his mother said in that mother's voice.

"Noooo," Aaron whined, leaning away.

Trevet tried again to pass the baby to his mother, without success. "It's okay," he said smilingly. "I'll put him in the chair."

Bri looked up at Trevet. He certainly is attractive when he smiles, she thought. Stop that! That was how you got into trouble with Tyrone, by noticing his charming smile. Not this time, she thought to herself, not this time. Bri mentally shook herself from admiring the man and sat while Trevet placed Aaron in the highchair.

When the order arrived, they ate in silence. Bri helped Aaron while he continued watching Trevet. Trevet noticed Bri picking at her food.

"You're not hungry?" he asked.

"No, not really."

"Nervous?" A little," she admitted. "They don't know I have a child."

"Call them, Bri, and talk to your mother," Trevet suggested, handing her his cell phone.

After a few minutes of talking on the phone, tears gathered in her eyes and slipped down her cheeks. "I love you too, Mom; see you soon," she replied in a tearful voice.

Trevet handed her a napkin. Bri handed him the phone. "Thank you, Mr. Harrison," she said, dabbing at her eyes.

"Can you call me, Trevet?" he asked. She nodded. Not long after lunch, they were back on the road. Aaron and Bri fell asleep.

Trevet glanced over at her. With her mouth slightly parted, she appeared so peaceful while she slept. He wondered how those perfect lips would feel on his. He visibly shook his head. What was he thinking? He didn't even like her. No matter how different she was from the young girl he had met a few years ago, he didn't want to feel any shred of attraction for her. He was doing a favor for Mr. Cleyvon, and that was it. He forced himself to focus on the road, only to glance at her again. He had to pull himself together. This was his employer's daughter. Trevet took a deep breath and forced his eyes away to concentrate on his driving. It seemed as if he'd been driving in North Carolina for hours. He needed to stop and stretch his legs for a while. He pulled into a rest area and turned off the engine to the car. He glanced at the baby and Bri, who were still asleep. His eyes lingered on her face. Bri Cleyvon had certainly grown up to be a beautiful woman. His eyes were trailing down her neck, wondering how it would feel to press his lips to the pulse that beat steadily. Gradually his eyes traveled to the swell of her full breasts that showed at the vee of her shirt. He had to stop this. Bri could be no more to him than his employer's daughter.

Nevertheless, Trevet reached out and gently caressed her cheek. Startled from sleep, Bri moved her head away so swiftly she bumped it hard on the window, which woke up Aaron. He started to cry. This was the second time he'd touched her and saw the same fear. What did Tyrone do to her?"

Holding the injured side of her head, Bri turned to her frightened son. "Shh … it's okay, baby," she cooed gently.

"I'm sorry," Trevet said sincerely. Bri looked at him, frowning and wondering why he'd touched her like that. Aaron's small arms reached for Trevet.

"Mama," Aaron whined. Bri looked at Trevet, who was staring at Aaron - dumbfounded. Bri started to laugh. Trevet's eyes shifted to stare at Bri.

"Mama," Aaron repeated, reaching for Trevet.

"Bri?" Trevet replied, and after a pause, started to laugh himself. Aaron stopped crying and looked from one to the other. Shaking his head, Trevet got out of the car and lifted Aaron from the car seat. With Bri beside him, Trevet carried the now-happy kid inside to the food court. This felt nice to him. Trevet smiled over at Bri.

"You should laugh more often," Trevet told her.

"I don't have much to laugh about anymore," she replied, looking up at him. She took Aaron to freshen him up and then joined Trevet outside the restroom. Right away, Aaron reached for Trevet, wanting nothing to do with his mother. "While it's still early, let's take Aaron to the zoo," Trevet said.

"Zoo? What zoo?" Bri asked. "Not far from here, in Asheville. Aaron will love it."

Bri said, shaking her head, "I don't know. Won't it make us late getting to Atlanta?"

"We could get a hotel room nearby and take off early in the morning." Aaron had one chubby arm around Trevet's neck, looking from him to his mother as if waiting for an answer. Bri shrugged.

"Okay, let's go." Bri was glad she agreed. Trevet and Aaron had a terrific time. She'd never heard Aaron laugh this much. She watched them and thought that Trevet would make an excellent father someday. Aaron walked between them, holding their hands.

"Why does he call me Mama?" Trevet asked.

"He doesn't know the name Daddy," she answered.

As the day wore on and when Aaron got tired, Trevet would swing him up on his shoulders. She looked over at Trevet, wondering if he ever married. She didn't see a ring. She was sure a man as beautiful as he was, was not without female companionship.

"You tired of him yet?" Bri asked. Most men shied away from children, and it surprised her how he had taken to Aaron and Aaron to him.

"No, I'm enjoying this," he admitted and honestly meant it.

It was easy to become attached to the little fellow riding his shoulders. They walked for a time and stopped often to look at the animals. They ate junk food and laughed, even Bri occasionally chuckled. Aaron was starting to get tired. When Bri reached for him, he turned away, putting both his chubby arms around Trevet's neck.

"He likes you, Mr. Harrison."

"Trevet. Call me Trevet," he interrupted.

It wasn't long before Aaron fell asleep in Trevet's arms. His small head lay on his shoulder while they walked back to the car.

"I'll take him," Bri said.

"It's okay." Trevet was surprised at how he was enjoying his time with Aaron and Bri. He hated to see it end. For a few hours, Bri had let her guard down and even joined to play with them. He opened the door for Bri and placed Aaron in his seat. Quietly they drove around

Asheville in search of an available hotel. It seems there was some sort of convention in town, so rooms were scarce.

They found a hotel with only one room available. Trevet didn't hesitate before taking the room. Aaron was so exhausted; he didn't awaken even while his mother changed him into his pajamas and laid him in the center of the bed. Bri showered, changed, and lay down beside the baby. "I'll sleep in the chair," Trevet told her.

"No, you can lay down with us," Bri offered. "It will be alright."

"Are you sure…?" Bri nodded before lying back down. Trevet went to the bathroom and returned with just his pants on, chest nude. With his back turned away from them, Bri used the opportunity to observe him. Her eyes roamed down his muscular body, acknowledging that he was all muscle. His broad shoulders and back tapered to a slim waist that flowed to a nice, hard backside and narrow hips. He had long, muscular, sturdy legs. When he moved, every muscle rippled. How she would love to sketch him in the nude or to feel the texture of his sculptured body beneath her hands. As if bewitched, Bri quietly rose from the bed and approached Trevet.

He turned and watched her walk toward him before stopping. She reached out to lightly touch his chest, allowing her fingers to move caressingly to his carved abs. Trevet stood still and quietly watched her. She didn't know what she was doing to him. He felt himself thicken at her gentle touch. Bri took a deep breath, and Trevet felt his heartbeat quicken. He watched as her tongue slowly moistened her lips. Finally, their eyes met. She gazed deeply into his gray eyes, and all conscious thought faded from her head as her fingertips traced the velvety planes of his chest.

"I would like to sketch you," she said softly, her heart beating rapidly.

New things were happening to her body. The touch of his hot body beneath her fingers made her feel things she had never felt before, things she had never felt with Tyrone.

Trevet liked the feel of her hands on him. Hooded gray eyes looked down at her.

"If I touch you, will you pull away?" he asked her huskily. Her head rose, and their eyes met. Bri heard him, but what he said didn't register. The longer she looked into his eyes, the more spellbound she became. Trevet reached out and pushed a strand of hair from her face. Bri stiffened, but she didn't pull away. Trevet's head lowered and yet she didn't move. Tentatively, his lips touched hers softly. What was meant to be a quick, gentle kiss turned into a deep, passion-filled, and soul-stirring event.

Trevet's fingers threaded through her hair, gently pulling her to him. He placed his free hand on her waist and pressed her against his throbbing body. He deepened the kiss, slipping his tongue past her lips and into her mouth. Her breath caught in her throat. Bri kissed him back as if she'd been waiting a lifetime to be kissed by a man like him. Lord knows Tyrone never kissed her like this, if at all. She slid her hands up his naked chest. He had soft lips and a skilled tongue that intoxicated her senses, making her feel lightheaded as her heart beat rapidly in her chest. Bri eased away and sighed. Her fingers touched her lips. She moved away then walked to the side of the bed and lay down.

"Goodnight," she said softly.

Trevet could still taste her lips against his and smell her unique scent. He stared at her, confused yet fascinated. Why did he kiss her, he asked himself? More importantly, a better question was why did she allow him to kiss her? He knew then that he had to stay clear of Bri Cleyvon; it would be so easy to fall for this changed Bri. He liked his life the way it was; free of commitment and the drama a relationship could bring. At the age of twenty-eight, he wasn't ready for a long-term relationship. He also knew deep in his heart that Bri could be the one to usurp his orderly lifestyle. Trevet looked at them asleep in the bed. In just a day, son and mother were getting under his skin. Turning away from the beautiful sight, he decided he had to stay clear of Bri Cleyvon and her son. He is taking them to her parents, and that would be that. What did he know about her anyway? All he remembered was that spoiled rich kid. He has only known this supposedly changed Bri for one day. As far as he knew, this new Bri could be an imposter, and when she is reunited with her parents, the old Bri could reveal herself. He frowned. Then why did he desire her so strongly? Granted, she was beautiful; but she still had issues to deal with, and he didn't need that sort of drama in his life right now.

Chapter Four

Trevet awoke to something pulling at his lashes. He opened one eye to see a small cherub face looking down at him, grinning.

"Mama."

"Good morning, Aaron," Trevet said, smiling at the boy. He looked over at Bri. She was on her side turned away from him, still asleep and softly snoring.

"We're going to have to find you a new name," he said, smiling and rising from the bed. Aaron crawled to the edge of the bed and reached for Trevet.

"You're wet. Where did your Mom put your pull-ups?" he said while picking Aaron up. He looked into a large blue bag and found them.

"How about a bath first," he told the boy. "Maybe by then Mama will be awake and can dress you." He had no idea how to take care of a toddler. Trevet undressed Aaron and carried him into the bathroom. Sitting Aaron on his knees, he filled the tub with water. To the child's delight, Trevet let him splash and frolic all he wanted before Trevet took a clean washcloth and began to bathe his small body. When the actual bathing began, Aaron started singing his alphabets. Aaron stopped singing, looking up at Trevet expectantly.

"Mama ting," Aaron babbled.

"You want me to sing?" Trevet asked incredulously. Who was he to deny the toddler? Trevet sang with Aaron, and they clapped their hands when the song was over. Trevet lost count of how many times they sang "the alphabet song" and "Itsy Bitsy Spider".

Bri awakened to the sound of a deep voice singing nursery rhymes. She listened for a moment and smiled. Quietly, she went to the door of the bathroom and peeked in. Trevet sat on the edge of the tub with Aaron wrapped in a towel. After drying him, Trevet lifted the happy, laughing Aaron in the air. When he brought him down, Aaron held onto Trevet's face, gave him a wet kiss then hugged him. Trevet's strong arms went around his little body. Aaron loved Trevet, Bri realized. That was odd because her son was normally skittish around strangers. Smiling, Bri pushed open the door.

"Mama," Aaron called, reaching for his mother. Trevet handed Aaron to her.

"Thank you," Bri said softly. Their eyes met. Trevet leaned over and kissed her gently on the mouth. Bri's head lowered. With Aaron in her arms, she left the bathroom. While she dressed Aaron, her head reeled, remembering last night and that unforgettable kiss she received from Trevet. What was wrong with her? Why had she allowed him to kiss her? She was starting to feel drawn to him. It didn't matter that technically she'd known him for years. In the

past, she saw him as an old man, even though he was only five or six years older than she was.

She remembered bringing her girlfriends to her father's office just so they could drool over

Trevet. At that time, she had eyes only for Tyrone. She didn't see what her friends found

attractive about him. Now she did. Bri closed her eyes and sighed. She was too vulnerable right

now to get involved with any man, especially Trevet. She refused to allow herself to become

attracted to Trevet. She just can't let it happen - not now, not ever. She'd let him kiss her, for

goodness sake. What was the attraction? He was handsome, no doubt. He was great with

Aaron, and Aaron loved Trevet. Maybe the appeal was because of her son. It was good they

will arrive in Atlanta today. After Trevet dropped them off at her parents, she won't see him

again. Anyway, she would be returning to Virginia Beach in a few weeks

.

Four hours later, they pulled into her parents' winding driveway. Aaron lay sleeping. Trevet

put the car in park, and Bri looked over at him. "I'm afraid," she said softly.

"You'll be fine. Your parents love you," he said reassuringly.

Bri lost herself in the gray depths of his eyes, believing him... knowing he was right.

"Come on, Bri," he said. "I'll get Aaron."

Bri sat awhile and took in her surroundings. Her childhood home hadn't changed much, she

thought. The large white, two-story antebellum house had tall colonnades extended around the

house. A roof over the portico covered the balcony on the second floor. Bri could remember

fondly sitting on the balcony outside the French doors of her bedroom, her legs dangling through

the rails. She loved this house and had a happy life here. She didn't realize how well she lived

until she defied her parents and ran off with Tyrone. Trevet took the sleeping child from his seat.

Bri joined him, and together they went to her parents' door. The door opened, and there stood Irene Cleyvon. She was a small, elegant woman with classic features. Her graying hair was pulled back in a bun. Bri fell into her mother's arms and wept. Irene held her close, thanking Trevet while she held onto her wayward daughter. Bri held her mother tightly.

"Oh, my baby," Irene cried, holding Bri close.

"Come inside," she invited with her arm around Bri's shoulders. Trevet followed them inside with a sleeping Aaron in his arms. They were led to a spacious living room; a living room Bri remembered. Aaron started to awaken and looked at his grandmother shyly, his head on Trevet's shoulder. Bri went to them.

"Aaron, this is Grandma," she gently told the baby. Aaron looked at her for a minute and then reached for her. Irene took him and held him tight, her eyes brimming with tears.

"Mom, how's Dad?" Bri asked.

"He's getting better. Let's go see him." The four of them went to the solarium in the back of the house. Jorge Cleyvon lay back on the lounger.

"Jorge," his wife called. Jorge turned to see Bri. His eyes filled as he surveyed his only child. His arms opened to her, and Bri ran to him, hugged him, and began to cry anew.

"Oh, Daddy," she choked out, "I'm sorry. I should have listened to you and Mom. I'm so ashamed."

"No, baby, it's over now, and we'll speak no more of this." He raised her face, looking at her intently with love in his eyes.

"My heart is full," Jorge said with a smile.

"How are you, Dad?"

"Better now," he said, stroking her hair. He looked over at Trevet. "Thank you, Son."

Trevet nodded. Jorge turned his attention to his grandson. "Bring him over, Mother, so I can see him."

Irene put Aaron down, and they walked to his grandfather. Bri looked over at Trevet and smiled; this time it reached her eyes. "Thank you, Trevet."

Trevet turned to leave. Aaron saw him. "Mama," he cried, running to Trevet.

Trevet lifted him. Aaron patted Trevet's face. Bri smiled. "He calls Trevet Mama," she informed her parents.

Trevet knew he had to leave but he hated to. He had grown quite fond of the little boy in such a brief time. Bri went to them and took Aaron from his arms. She looked up at him. "I know you have to leave," she spoke softly. "Thank you, Trevet, for everything." He smiled down at her.

"I enjoyed the drive," he replied. "Bye, Aaron," he said, waving to the boy.

Aaron's little face frowned and he reached for Trevet.

Trevet took his fingers and kissed them. Turning, he left them, and Aaron let out a wail. "Mama!" Aaron screamed loudly. Bri tried to soothe him. Trevet's heart went out to him, but he knew he had to go. He didn't look back and could hear Aaron screaming. When he reached for the doorknob, he stopped. He walked back into the house to the solarium; he could hear Aaron still crying. He saw Trevet and stretched for him.

Trevet took him. "Shh…" he cooed while Aaron held on to him tightly.

Bri looked at her parents. "He fell in love with Trevet," she said smiling.

"I can stay for a while," he informed them and took Aaron to the backyard. Bri watched from the solarium as Aaron ran around in the yard.

"Baby," her father stated, "how have you been?"

"I'm all right, Dad, or I will be."

"Still painting?" Bri nodded.

"Sit," he said, "We need to talk." Bri and Irene sat across from her father.

"Bri, I have prostate cancer. I'm going through the treatments, and I feel I'm getting better, thank God. Your mother takes very good care of me. I needed to find you, Daughter, just in case. I didn't want to leave without telling you that I love you very much." Jorge paused. "Everything that has happened was not your fault; I handled it all wrong. I never disowned you. I spoke in anger, so please forgive me."

"Daddy, it's not your fault. I did this to myself. I wanted to come home so badly. I know I hurt you and Mom," she said, taking her mother's hand in hers. "I was ashamed. Tyrone… well he kept a tight rein on me." Her head lowered. "How did you finally get away?" her mother asked. She took a deep breath.

"He beat me, many times. We moved around so much, half the time I didn't know where we were. Then when I got pregnant, he was violently angry. When I refused to have an abortion, he began to beat me more. I guess he thought to make me miscarry, but Aaron survived. After Aaron's birth, I knew it was time for me to get away, anyway that I could. So, while he was in his drugged haze, I took Aaron and ran. We settled in Virginia Beach. I filed for divorce. The times they found him, he refused to sign the papers. I will probably be stuck with Tyrone the rest of my life. I haven't seen him since running away that night."

"Don't worry, Bri," her father said. "I'll get Trevet to work on it. He'll get him to sign; he'll do whatever it takes to get his signature."

"I don't know where he is Dad," Bri informed him.

"He's in Atlanta," Jorge regrettably told her. "He came here a few months ago looking for you and accused us of hiding you."

Bri was immediately alarmed. "Dad, I have to leave here. At least in Virginia Beach, he couldn't find us," she said, feeling the fear rise in her.

"Calm down, baby. He won't come near you. I saw to that. Trevet will get your divorce finalized, and then you and little Aaron can live your life wherever you want. Maybe you'll want to come home for good." Bri hugged her father, knowing he was right. He would take care of everything. She could stay in Atlanta a while longer, just until her divorce was final; then she would return to Virginia.

Chapter Five

Bri sat on the balcony outside her bedroom, her legs dangling over the side. She couldn't forget the night Trevet kissed her. Why did he kiss her, she wondered, as she touched her lips? If she closed her eyes and concentrated, she could almost feel the warmth of his mouth pressed to hers. She hadn't seen Trevet for a few weeks or so. Her father informed her that he was working on the divorce, as promised. Occasionally, Aaron would cry for him; it amazed her how attached he had become to Trevet. She knew she would eventually have to consult with him. She looked up at the stars twinkling brightly in the Atlanta sky. She wondered what he was doing. Probably on a date, she thought. She was only with him that one time. She did see him one day in the Buckhead area of Atlanta, hand in hand with a beautiful woman. She felt a twinge of jealousy. She shouldn't be having any feelings towards him anyway. She was due to see him tomorrow to go over the progress of the divorce. She decided to take Aaron so he could see Trevet. She hoped he didn't mind.

Next morning, she sat outside his office with Aaron on her lap. The door opened and there he was. Aaron slid from her lap and ran to Trevet, who lifted him in the air. It was a pleasant surprise to see his young friend, and Aaron hugged his neck.

"Hello, Bri," he said over Aaron's head. Bri smiled.

"Come on in," he said, carrying Aaron with him. Bri followed, noting how different the office looked. Before her father retired, he was partial to the traditional design. Trevet preferred a contemporary look, which suited him. Bri took a seat in the chair in front of his desk. Aaron sat on his lap behind the desk and watched them with a smile on his handsome face.

"Aaron missed you," she said softly. Trevet smiled at her. "I missed him too," Trevet said, looking at the little boy.

When Jorge asked him to settle Bri's divorce, he didn't hesitate to complete this task. He thought of her often over the weeks, more than he cared to admit. His declaration of staying away from her flew out the window. For some reason, it didn't upset him as much as it should have. It was time to get down to business.

"Bri, you will have to see Tyrone when we meet with his attorney and discuss his demands to ensure that the divorce goes through. I've spoken to his lawyer." Trevet took a deep breath before continuing. "Tyrone is demanding alimony from you. He also threatened to sue you for custody of Aaron." Bri became alarmed. "How much?"

"Twenty-five grand a year," Trevet informed her. "Give it to him only if he gives up his parental rights to my son," she stated firmly. "Why is he demanding this?"

"He doesn't want to pay child support, not that any court would give him sole custody with his unsavory past. He could still get joint custody and demand visitation rights, which would be his right as Aaron's father."

"I don't want him anywhere near my son," she replied adamantly. "Can't you stop him?"

"Don't worry; he'll give up his rights gladly."

"Are you sure?"

"Positive, Bri, trust me," he reassured her. "Tomorrow at ten o'clock we'll meet with him." She nodded. "Come on, Aaron," she told her son.

"Noooo," Aaron whined, holding onto Trevet. Trevet smiled at his young friend. "Let me take you two to lunch," he invited. Bri smiled and agreed, finding she didn't want to leave him either. At the restaurant, Trevet watched as Bri fed Aaron what he missed. He was glad to see them. Many times, he wanted to stop by and see the baby - or was it Bri he wanted to see? It didn't matter. He did miss Aaron, and he couldn't forget the mother either.

He'd seen her one day in Buckhead and wanted to stop and talk, but he was with another woman. Why he felt uncomfortable with her seeing him with woman, as if he were cheating on her, was beyond him. But that's what he felt like when he saw her. He hadn't dated since. He looked at her and shook his head, as the realization of his feelings came to him. He wanted to see Bri; he wanted to be with Aaron. He decided he wouldn't fight it anymore; he would see her more and often. Satisfied with his decision, he smiled.

****

Trevet and Bri sat at a large table, facing Tyrone and his lawyer. Tyrone sat there looking smug and arrogant, glaring at Bri. She refused to look at him. Trevet spoke first.

"Ms. Cleyvon has agreed to a lump sum alimony payment if your client signs over his parental rights to their son," Trevet stated resolutely.

"He's my son too," Tyrone said. Bri raised her head to glare at Tyrone. "You could care less about him, Tyrone!" Bri shouted at him.

Tyrone smirked. "He's still my son." Bri met his eyes. "You're a bastard," she stated.

"Well, dear wife, if you want your divorce and the rights to my son, I need another fifty grand," he said smugly.

Bri's mouth fell open, and her eyes widened in surprise and disgust. She looked at Trevet with despair in her eyes then leaned to him and whispered, "What do I do?"

"You trust me?" He looked directly into her eyes. She looked at him for a moment and nodded. If her father trusts him, she could also.

"Mr. Grant, we will accept your request, with the understanding that this is all you will receive. In addition, you will have no contact with Bri or Aaron. As for the child, he knows nothing about you, and it will remain that way. A permanent no-contact order will be placed in the courts. You are not to return demanding more funds after you receive this one-time alimony payment; is that understood?" Trevet pulled out the papers and slid them to Tyrone's lawyer. His lawyer handed them to Tyrone, who looked over the divorce decree and noticed a $100,000 amount typed on the papers.

Tyrone looked up at Trevet, confused. "How did you know I'd up the amount?" Tyrone asked snidely.

"I know your kind, Mr. Grant," Trevet said arrogantly, extending his pen to him.

"What if I don't accept this?" Bri put her hand on Trevet's arm. She tensed, looking at him worriedly. "Then, Mr. Grant," Trevet said calmly, "we go to court. There will be an investigation into your character and into your activities of the past three years or so. Any criminal acts or discrepancies will be brought out in court, and you, Mr. Grant, will see repercussions for those actions - and you get nothing." Trevet's face was stern and unreadable.

Tyrone snatched the pen from Trevet and signed quickly. Trevet looked at his signature, opened his briefcase, and handed Tyrone a cashier's check.

"Yes!" Tyrone said, moving from the table. "Have a nice life, Bri," he stated and left the room.

Bri sighed loudly, her hand still on Trevet's arm. She looked up at Trevet's handsome face.

"Thank you, Trevet. I don't know how else to thank you," she said with a feeling of euphoria flowing through her. She was free and wanted to shout for joy. Trevet's hand covered hers.

"Have dinner with me tonight?" he asked.

Bri smiled. "I'd like that." "Eight then?" Bri nodded.

Chapter Six

Bri admired herself in the full-length mirror. The candy red Givenchy dress fit her petite frame perfectly. The thin straps attached to the bodice of the dress hugged her breast, giving them a slight lift. The middle of the dress hugged her tiny waist while the skirt of the dress swirled around her shapely legs. Red Kenneth Cole pumps completed her ensemble. Her shoulder length hair brushed her shoulders. She smiled, pleased with her appearance. When she went downstairs, Trevet held Aaron as he read his favorite book.

As she entered the living room, Bri stopped in the archway with a loving smile on her beautiful face, touched by what she saw. She would love to paint the picture that was before her. Aaron's young adoring eyes gazed into Trevet's face, hanging on his every word while Trevet looked down at the book; he occasionally glanced over at Aaron. The adoration in her son's eyes made her misty. Aaron's eyes were starting to get heavy, and he fought hard to keep them open. If she weren't sure of it before, she certainly was now: Aaron loves Trevet. If any child deserved a father, it was her adorable boy. However, she wasn't sure if that was healthy for her son, and tonight she would speak to Trevet about Aaron's attachment. She refused to allow Aaron's heart to be broken when Trevet no longer had a reason to come around. Irene joined her, smiling as she stood beside Bri.

"Isn't that a lovely sight?" her mother said. Bri smiled and nodded. Irene's eyes looked over at her daughter. "You look beautiful, baby. Have a good time because you deserve it." Bri kissed her mother's cheek.

"Thanks, I will Mom." Aaron finally lost the battle, and his eyes slowly closed. Trevet set the book aside, rose, and carried Aaron to his room. Bri followed close behind him. She watched as Trevet gently lay her son down, leaned, and kissed his forehead. Trevet turned to her.

"Ready?" Bri nodded.

Trevet stopped and let his eyes journey from her beautiful face to her tiny feet. The blood flowing through him heated, settling in his groin. "You're beautiful," he complimented softly. Taking her hand, he led her down the stairs. "Thank you, Trevet. You look quite handsome yourself," she smiled up at him. The taupe Armani suit he wore made him look as if he'd stepped off the cover of GQ magazine. The supper club was one of Atlanta's premier nightspots, famous for the blues and jazz bands that perform there.

Once inside, the Maitre'D immediately led them to their table in one of the most intimate parts of the restaurant. After seating Bri, Trevet took his seat across from her. The wine steward was two steps behind the maître d'. Trevet looked over the wine list and ordered a bottle of their best wine. After the wine steward left, their server appeared and filled their water glasses before offering menus, reciting the dinner specials, and leaving. Bri's eyes scanned the interior of the restaurant. She had heard many praiseworthy things about this restaurant when she lived in Atlanta but never had the opportunity to dine here.

"This place is great," Bri commented as she looked around at the décor of the room.

"I've been here a few times. The food and the service are excellent." Trevet confirmed.

The wine arrived. After Trevet tasted it for approval, the waiter filled each glass to the proper level and left the bottle in the bucket beside the table.

Bri tasted her wine and was surprised. "This is really good." She watched as he lifted his glass and sipped, nodding his agreement. Lowering her head, Bri gazed at her menu. When she lifted her head, she met his beautiful gray eyes, and her heart slammed in her chest. They stared at each other across the table for a moment, neither of them ready to break the silence. A current flowed between them, strong and vibrant. Thankfully, the server returned to take their orders, and the moment was lost.

"I can't thank you enough for helping me to get rid of Tyrone," she commented before taking another sip of wine and setting the glass back down. Trevet filled her glass again. Bri lifted it and took another sip.

"There is no need for thanks; I would do anything for Mr. and Mrs. Cleyvon, you and Aaron."

It amazed him the difference in Bri. She was not the same person she was all those years ago. That spirited yet spoiled young woman was gone, and in her place, was a beautiful, deep but unhappy woman. It made him wonder what she went through with Tyrone. He wanted to see her smiling and happy again as she was when they took Aaron to the zoo.

"Do you still plan to return to Virginia Beach now that Tyrone is out of your life?" he inquired nonchalantly before lifting his glass of wine. Please stay, he wished silently.

She shrugged. It's still open," she answered. "I want to make sure Dad is better. Eventually I have to return. I have some commissioned work to complete."

The first course of their meal arrived, and the conversation moved around to summer festivals that were coming and the places she thought Aaron would enjoy seeing. As the other courses followed, Trevet couldn't help comparing her to the women he'd dated in the past. He never talked as easily with them as he did Bri. Their conversations jumped from politics to current events with such ease it fascinated him. He never knew one so young had so much depth.

As the meal came and went, Bri felt herself relaxing more and more with Trevet, or could it be the wine she consumed? The band performing tonight had a female lead singer whose voice was beautiful and complimented the romantic setting and intimate ambiance of the room. Bri felt a freedom she had not felt for a very long time. The conversation they shared was light and airy, exactly how she felt this night. She was glad she had come out with Trevet. A wall of silence developed between them when couples started to dance. Trevet took her hand and led her to the floor. The band played an old Etta James song '*Trust in Me."* Trevet gracefully moved her to the music, causing her to feel a comfort in his arms she had never felt. She sighed, closed her eyes, and laid her head on his chest. She loved the feel of Trevet's arms around her, the way his strong hands held her hand to his chest as he swayed with her. So, engrossed in him, she didn't hear the change in the music. Trevet gently pushed her away and turned her with one hand.

Surprised by this move and before she could gasp, she found herself back into his arms. She laughed a girlish giggle as he easily moved her around the dance floor. It surprised Bri that a man tall as he could be so graceful. When the song ended, he led her back to the table.

"You're a terrific dancer" she complimented.

"I love to dance," he admitted. Trevet smiled, watching her as she smiled into his eyes. This is the first time since he found her that he has ever seen her so relaxed and carefree.

"You should laugh more often; it's a beautiful sound."

Bri's head lowered. Trevet reached out with his finger and lifted her chin. "Why do you lower your head?" he asked quietly.

"I didn't realize I did," she said softly, looking into his eyes and slowly losing all logical thought.

Her eyes strayed to his perfect, chiseled mouth and remembered his kiss, secretly wishing he would kiss her again. Her heart raced from the memory.

"Another dance?" he asked, extending his hand. She slipped her small hand into his large hand and allowed him to lead them to the dance floor. They swayed to a rendition of *Kenny G's "Songbird"* with her head on his chest. She could hear the steady beat of his heart in her ear. With her eyes closed, she exhaled. Trevet loved the feel of her small body in his arms. Her fresh, clean scent, with a hint of powder, intoxicated him; if he were not careful, he could fall for Bri Cleyvon very easily. She sighed again, and he felt her hand tighten on his back, pulling herself closer to him. He looked down at her head on his chest. Feeling his eyes on her, she lifted her head. Their eyes met. Her eyes lowered to his mouth, and she leaned into him unconsciously.

"You know not what you do, my lady," Trevet stated seductively. Her lips parted slightly. His head lowered and gently kissed her lips. She moved closer to him. She pulled her hand from his, wrapped her arms around his neck, and rose up on her toes, while still moving to the music. Trevet lifted his head; his gray eyes were dark with passion as he gazed at her face. Her eyes closed, and she moaned softly. That was Trevet's undoing. He had to get her away from him because, at that exact moment, he wanted her more than he had ever wanted a woman.

"Bri," he said softly. Her eyes opened.

"I better take you home," he suggested. Bri frowned with disappointment in her eyes. Maybe he didn't want to be with her the way she wanted to be with him, she thought.

"Not yet," she replied softly, boldly.

"Okay," Trevet said, pulling her closer to him. He wasn't ready to leave yet. He was loving too much the feel of her in his arms. He couldn't understand the feelings he had for her. It's only been a few months since their first meeting. What was happening? The emotions he felt for her were too fast, but he'd be damned if he stopped them. He just needed to slow things down for now. Bri didn't want this night to end. She sighed and laid her head on his chest. They danced to three more songs; sometimes they were the only couple on the floor.

He was bringing emotions out in her that she thought were long gone. She didn't quite understand what it was she felt. Was this how it felt when you desired a man, she wondered. The dawning came suddenly. She wanted him. She wanted him to make love to her. She wanted to feel the fire she saw in his eyes, to know what it felt like to have a man like Trevet make love to her. It didn't matter that they had just met; right now, she wanted to feel his body beside her, stroking her, and beneath her hands. She raised her head. Their eyes met. "Take me to your place."

His breath caught in his throat. "I don't think that's a good idea."

"Why?"

"If I…" Trevet paused, looking into her deep brown eyes at the passion he saw smoldering there. Bri's mouth ached to be kissed.

"Are you sure?"

"I've never been surer of anything in my life," she stated firmly.

****

At his home, Trevet took her shawl and told her to take a seat while he got refreshments for them. Bri took a shaky breath and hoped she wasn't making yet another mistake in her life by being alone with Trevet. Her eyes scanned his living room. The room was beautiful and elegantly designed with a masculine flair. Everything was made to accommodate his large size. The chairs that surrounded the fireplace in the room were large and extremely comfortable looking. The glass and chrome pieces accented the room perfectly. A few minutes later, Trevet returned with two glasses of wine in his hand. Handing one to her, he took a seat beside her on the large sofa. Bri smiled her thanks.

"Trevet, do you have a girlfriend?" Bri broke the uncomfortable silence.

"No, I date," he answered honestly.

"Don't you ever want to marry?" He shrugged. "Someday, I guess," he answered, wondering why she asked so many questions.

"Bri, why all the questions?" "I don't know," she answered and sipped her wine. "I've never been alone with a man before, other than Tyrone. I guess I'm a little nervous."

"Don't be; nothing will happen unless you want it to," he said assuring her. Her head lowered.

He raised her chin and looked deeply into her dark eyes. "What is it that you do to me, Bri?" he thought aloud.

"Do you still love Tyrone?"

"No," she said honestly. "I don't think I ever loved him," she admitted. Taking a deep breath, Bri felt the need to disclose all she went through with Tyrone, only if to make him understand why she was the person she is now.

Bri took another sip of wine. "He was horrible to me. He beat me it seemed all the time," she told him. She visibly saw Trevet's body tense. She reached her hand out and touched his arm; she could feel his muscles tense under her hands. "It's alright now. He is out of my life forever," she reassured him. Looking at him, she tilted her head to the side. "You know what I hated the most about Tyrone? The way he would take me; anytime and anywhere he wanted. Just jump on me like some rutting hog; I hated it and I hated him. The only good thing was conceiving Aaron." Trevet didn't comment. He just listened as she talked. He was glad she was losing some of her fear now that Tyrone was out of her life. She is so damned cute, he thought, with her dulcet tone and gentle smile. "That's because you have never been made love to, Bri," he told her. "When the right one comes along, you'll know what it really is." Her head lowered. "Will you show me what it's like?" She asked so softly, he barely heard her. When he didn't respond, she raised her head, her eyes gazing into his.

"Bri, are you sure you want this?"

"Yes," she whispered.

"Show me how enjoyable it can be, Trevet. I've never felt that. I want to know what it's like to feel passion, to feel the touch of your hands or just to be held."

He leaned toward her and pulled her head to him. His lips touched hers. Her mouth parted after feeling his sweet breath on her lips. His tongue slid into her mouth. Little spasms of pleasure darted through her now and made her aware of a strange little twinge of need between her thighs. She'd never experienced anything so glorious. She slipped her arms around his neck, returning the kiss. Trevet's lips left her mouth and rained light kisses to her neck before moving to the swell of her breasts above her dress. Bri's head lolled back, and she moaned softly, loving the feel of his mouth on her. Where his lips touched her skin, a sensation went through her body so intense, she gasped. Trevet raised his head, and their eyes met.

She touched his lips, tracing her fingertip over his lips. "You have a beautiful mouth," she stated breathlessly. This time she kissed him. Her tongue entered his mouth and lingered; she moaned when his tongue touched hers. Trevet lifted his head and looked deep into her eyes before his mouth covered hers, kissing her hard. He brought her so close to him that he laid back on the couch with her on top of him. She twined her arms around his neck. Her legs then parted, and she came into direct connection with his growing manhood. She kissed him just as passionately as he did her. She flexed her hips, grinding against him, and he groaned. She was on the edge of an orgasm right then. Trevet grasped her hips to stop her before he came. Easing her off him, he rose and took her hand before pulling her with him. He couldn't stop himself from caressing her as he led her to the bedroom. Still clothed, Trevet coaxed her to sit on the bed. He lowered himself to her feet and removed her shoes. Bri moved to the center of the bed. Trevet kicked off his shoes and lay beside her.

Trevet leaned over her, and she looked directly into his now steel gray eyes. His mouth was so near, their breaths mingled. He kissed her. She sighed. He traced her lips with his tongue. She sighed.

"Meet me," he said into her mouth. Her head rose to take what he offered so freely. Trevet's mouth trailed hot kisses down her neck to the swell of her breasts. Bri's breath caught in her throat. Her small hands touched the back of his head and trailed to his broad shoulders; the muscles rippled under her hands. Trevet leaned up and gazed into her eyes.

"I want to feel you under my hands," she said, pulling at his shirt. He got up and pulled his shirt off his broad shoulders. Bri sat up anxiously, waiting to see his body again. When he was shirtless, she scooted to the edge of the bed and touched his bare chest. He was beautiful. Where her hands touched, so did her lips. Trevet moaned at the touch of her warm, gentle hands caressing him. Laying her down, Trevet stood over her. Slowly his hands stroked her legs and traveled up under her dress. His hand trailed up to her underwear, and his finger slipped into the side of her panties, teasing her by barely touching her. His steely gray eyes held hers. His finger rubbed her sensual spot. She moaned, and her legs opened and arched against his hand instinctively. His finger slipped inside her wetness, and her walls tightened. Trevet hissed at the tightness he felt. Reluctantly, he removed his fingers. If he didn't take her now, he was going to burst. He wanted to be inside her, to feel the tightening of her walls as he'd felt on his finger. He left her to remove the rest of his clothing. Bri reached behind her, unzipped her dress, and tossed it on the side of the bed. She unhooked the bra and let it fall to the floor. Bri lay before him clad only in her hi-cut, red lace panties.

She was everything he thought she'd be: sexy, incredibly shapely and damn she smelled so good. Bri admired his body. He was magnificent. His sculptured body fascinated her and she wanted to run her hands all over him. She felt his weight on the bed as he joined her and lay at her side. His lips found hers; she knew she could kiss him forever. His strong hands cupped her breasts, gently kneading them until her nipples were like pebbles. When his lips left hers, he took the nub in his mouth and Bri sighed loudly. Gently he sucked, flicking his tongue over the nipple and switching to imbibe the other breast with the same wonderful treatment. The excitement that went through her caused her to gasp from the sensation. She had never felt anything like it. Her hand grasped his head, not holding but stroking his head as he drove her insane with his hot skillful mouth. His lips trailed down to her flat stomach, and her stomach contracted under his lips. He moved lower. Bri tensed and grabbed the blankets, feeling his

breath on her most intimate part.

"Trevet," she cried. His mouth was even with her femininity. He kissed her nub chastely,

feeling her body shudder. He continued placing kisses over her, her gasps and cries making him

even more aroused than he already was. He was too far gone to pull away. She tasted so

delicious, so pure, and so womanly. He lifted her hips and drank his fill of her as her hot

wetness burst forth between her thighs.

"Trevet," she moaned. Her body tingled in the most incredible way from her head to the tip

of her toes. His tongue was wreaking havoc on her body. He rose above her and pushed her

knees apart. She looked up at him in a daze.

"I want to make you feel like I feel," she said huskily.

"You will," he replied as he reached over to the side table, got a condom, and rolled it over

his rock hard shaft. She was ready, and he couldn't wait anymore. Trevet positioned himself

between her thighs then took her mouth, demanding her attention. Swirling his shaft around her

nub between her swollen folds, he allowed the crown to enter her tight slit.

"Open for me, baby," he growled. When her legs opened wide, he thrust forward. She

screamed and dug her nails into his back. Trevet stilled, hissing at the sensation, and savoring

the wet tightness of her. He took pleasure in the way she pulsated around his hardened manhood.

Slowly he moved in her as she moved beneath him, her mouth gently nipping and sucking on his

neck. Lifting one thigh, he tunneled deep inside her, and she screamed her pleasure as she

clamped around him like a vise. Repeatedly he buried his manhood in her, riding her like a man

possessed. Bri met him thrust for thrust, stroke for stroke, holding him in a tight embrace as she

rode the storm that was building between them. Lust tore through him like molten lava. His hand reached between them and caressed her nub while he moved inside her; it was her undoing. He removed his hand and knew she was finding her peak, and he was losing control with her wild abandonment. Trevet leaned on his hands with his head back and eyes closed as he felt her orgasm massaging his manhood. The muscles in his arms contracted and bulged as he moved inside her, pushing in and out of her unabashedly. Then desire consumed him as she screamed her release that echoed in the room. He wanted this ecstasy to last forever. Trevet lay atop her, his face in the side of her neck and their bodies still entangled. Both regained the energy they had given with each other. Bri lay staring dazed at the ceiling, in awe of what she had just experienced. Trevet rolled from her and lay on his side. She turned her head, looking at him with a smile playing on her lips that turned into a broad grin.

"So," he said smiling, "What are you grinning about?"

Bri rolled away, hiding her face in the pillow. Trevet couldn't resist caressing her naked behind. She turned back to face him. He had a smug look on his face; he knew he had pleased her.

"Did I please you?" she asked hesitantly. Her hand caressed his chest and journeyed lower to his hard abdomen then continued downward until she held him in her hand. She felt him throb at her touch. She looked at him. His eyes closed with a groan. Still holding on to him, she leaned into him and placed her lips on his chest.

"I love your hands on me; don't stop," he said low.

Gently she pushed him to his back and straddled him. She leaned forward and kissed him. She lifted her mouth.

"Help me to please you," she said against his lips.

He lifted her hips and eased her down on him. "Oh my," he heard her say, and he smiled.

"I'm going to enjoy you, my lady, and I guarantee you're going to enjoy me," he said while he moved inside her. They made love through the night and slept until mid-morning.

Chapter Seven

Bri woke, startled. "Oh no!" she cried, bounding from the bed hastily. "What time is it?" she asked in alarm, looking on the floor for her clothes. She found her dress and slipped it on, zipping it up. Leaning up on his elbow, Trevet watched as she frantically looked around the floor.

"Where are my panties?"

"Bri," Trevet called calmly.

She palmed her breasts in her hands. "Oh my, did I wear a bra?"

"Bri," Trevet repeated, a smile playing on his lips.

"Why are you lying there?" she said, finding one shoe and slipping it on her foot. "Where is my other shoe?" she said, hobbling around with one pump on her foot.

"Oh my, Aaron's going to miss me."

"Bri, will you calm down." Trevet started laughing at her.

She stopped moving and frowned at him, hands on hips. "Trevet!" she yelled. "Get out of that bed!" she demanded.

Trevet fell back on the bed, laughing harder. She hobbled to the side of his bed and snatched the covers from him.

"Stop that and get out of that bed!"

"Bri, it's okay. I called your parents. Aaron is fine. You're..." he told her.

"Oh, Trevet, you didn't," she groaned, covering her face.

Trevet laughed harder and pulled her down on him.

"Trevet," she said in a warning tone. He unzipped her dress; her arms went behind to stop him. "Trevet, stop that!" she said. "I have to go!"

"Not today," he said, nibbling on her ear.

"Stop it, Trevet. I mean it" she said softly, trying to pull away from him. He held her to him with one arm across her back. His free hand caressed her rounded butt.

"You have to stop," she said, weakening, before his lips took hers. She relaxed against him.

"No," she gasped with her eyes closed. His hands were doing things she couldn't explain or resist. He rolled her over and hovered over her.

"Aaron is fine; your parents know you're with me."

"Yeah, and now they know what we were doing last night," she groaned and covered her face with her hands.

"You think," he said, trying to sound surprised. Bri removed her hands and glared at him.

He quickly kissed her. "So, if I'm to spend this day with you, what are we going to do first?"

"That's simple. I'm going to ravish you, bathe you, ravish you again, feed you, and ravish you again. Then we will pick up Aaron and take him to the park and dinner. Bri smiled and kissed him.

****

Hours later, Bri and Trevet arrived at her parents' house. Everyone was in the back yard. Aaron saw Trevet.

"Daddy!" he cried, happily running to him. Trevet picked him up. Trevet looked at Bri and mouthed Daddy, frowning. Bri shrugged, shaking her head. Bri went to her parents and kissed them.

"Dad, you look good today," she said.

"And you're glowing," he whispered. "Isn't she Mother?" Irene winked.

"I should say so, Dad." Bri blushed and went to greet her son.

"Mama," Aaron said happily. "Hey, have you been a good boy?" she asked, smiling at her adorable son. "Yes," he lisped. Trevet winked at Bri, smiling.

"Daddy, no go bye-bye," Aaron said, looking at Trevet. Trevet looked at Bri and smiled. Aaron clasped his face between his little hands, gaining his attention.

"Daddy, no bye-bye," he repeated.

"No, Aaron, no bye-bye," Trevet repeated and hugged Aaron. Bri's hand rested on Trevet's arm.

"Give Mama a kiss," Trevet told Aaron. He leaned over and gave his mother a wet kiss.

"Daddy kisses Mama," Aaron said to Trevet. Trevet smiled; Bri frowned.

Trevet leaned down to kiss Bri's lips. "Mm…that's good," he whispered and smiled when they parted. Bri blushed and went to change.

Jorge called Trevet over. Trevet sat beside him. "She's fragile, Trevet. Don't hurt her."

Trevet didn't know if it was advice or a warning. "I have no intention of that, Jorge. I really care about her."

53

"Good," he said, smiling. "Now, if anything should happen to me…" "Jorge dear, please," Irene said. Jorge took his wife's hand in his.

"Mother," he said looking at her with love.

"If anything should happen to me, I want you to take care of my family," Jorge requested of him.

"I'd be honored," Trevet told him honestly.

"Jorge, must you speak of this now? It upsets me," Irene said, her eyes welling up with tears.

"Mother, I have to make sure you and Bri are taken care of," he said, bringing her hand to his lips.

Irene smiled at him. "You rascal," she said adoringly.

Trevet watched them. He wished for the love they shared. After 30 years of marriage, they were still madly in love.

Irene smiled at Trevet. "Trevet you know we love you as if you were our own son and we trust you, but tread lightly with Bri. She's been hurt, and her self-esteem is extremely low; however, I think you and Bri would be happy together, plus you have a son, Dad."

Trevet smiled. He liked the idea of that. He loved Aaron. Trevet glanced over at him playing with his ball. Aaron looked up, smiled, and ran to Trevet. Trevet scooped him up and hugged him. Jorge and Irene looked at each other and smiled.

****

Trevet and Bri were sitting on the balcony outside her room. Her eyes looked at the stars twinkling in the dark sky. Trevet noticed how quiet Bri had been for the past couple of days, having spent almost every day together. His greatest joy was coming to see her and Aaron. They hadn't made love since the first time, by his choice. He needed to slow things down with her. Things were just happening too fast. It wasn't that he didn't want her; damn, he wanted her all the time. He'd thought about her constantly these few months she had been in Atlanta. Right now, he needed to be sure she was what he wanted and she was sure he was the man for her. She had been in Atlanta for six months now, and he knew she had a life in Virginia Beach. Was he the reason she'd stayed as long as she had? He wasn't sure. He didn't want her to leave Atlanta, but eventually he knew she had to return to Virginia.

"Bri," Trevet said. Her eyes met his then she lowered her head. Trevet lifted her chin.

"You've been quiet lately. Is something wrong?" He looked directly into her eyes. She pulled her face away, rose, and walked to the other side of the balcony. Trevet frowned and went to her. Her back was to him, and her hands tensely grasped the railing. He exhaled a deep breath and went to stand behind her, close but not touching.

Bri stared out into the night. Why didn't he want her anymore, she wondered? He hadn't tried to touch her, just a brotherly kiss on the cheek. Didn't he want her, as she desired him? Late at night, she could still feel him inside her. She wanted him to hold her and make love to her as he'd done before. Every time she saw him, her heart rate increased, and an excited joy would envelop her. Granted they had fun together with Aaron. She enjoyed the time he spent with him, but he never showed her any affection. Trevet had awakened something in her, and she wanted to hold on to it with both hands. Did he use her? No. If he did, he wouldn't continue to come to see Aaron. So why? Is what they shared all there was to it? Maybe she wasn't what he wanted.

If that were the case, she'd made a mistake and fell in love with the wrong person again. Bri turned to face him and looked into his gray eyes. She stepped to him, placed her hands on his chest. She felt him tense; therefore, she dropped her hands and moved away from him. She stopped and turned to him. "Just tell me, Trevet," she said.

"What, Bri?"

"What we shared meant nothing to you," she said, taking a shaky breath. "The mistake I made was making more of it than it really was; how naïve of me."

"Bri, it's not that it didn't mean anything. It's just things are happening too fast."

"Too fast," she repeated. "You're right. Thanks for being kind about it."

"Bri, you have to understand, it's not…" he started.

Bri raised her hand. "There's no need to explain. I understand." She turned to go into her room and then stopped. "I'm going home tomorrow," she said and turned to leave him.

"Bri! Come back here!" Trevet felt his heart skip a beat. She can't just leave, not yet. He needed more time with her; she needed more time with him. Damn it, he thought.

Bri turned. "Why, Trevet? I have work to do; I stayed longer than I had planned. Anyway, it's time. Goodnight, Trevet." She left him alone on the balcony.

Bri watched through her window as Trevet got into his car and left. The tears that had been burning at the back of her eyes flowed down her face. She wanted him. She loved him, but he didn't love her.

Trevet sat in the oversized chair, still damp from his shower and naked under his robe, wondering what had just happened. He had to take things slow with Bri; he had to be sure she knew the difference between lust and love. He knew she wanted him, but he had to slow down. He had to be sure. He wanted her; there was no doubt about that. They made him feel complete when he was with them. He felt as if Bri and Aaron were his family, and he wanted true love to go with the family.

Chapter Eight

Bri threw herself into her painting. In the two months she had returned to Virginia Beach, she had two scheduled exhibits. Her paintings had become so popular that the Virginia Beach Tourist Committee wanted to feature an article in their travel brochure and have a small showing when the tourist season started in a few months. Then to her surprise, she got a call from a well-known gallery in New York with a proposal to display her artwork, which she was seriously thinking about doing. Trevet was constantly on her mind. On occasion, he would call and ask about her and Aaron, who missed him terribly. When Trevet finished talking to him, her poor baby would cry. Sometimes she felt like crying herself. She had to get herself together and stop pining for something that never had a chance of happening.

Bri and Aaron were eating breakfast. "Mama," Aaron said, "I see Daddy?" Aaron had asked that question every day since they had returned to Virginia. She knew Aaron missed Trevet; she missed him too. Nevertheless, he has his own life; he owed nothing to her or to Aaron. The times she had spoken to her father, he told her Trevet was working endlessly. Her mother informed her that she thought Trevet missed her and Aaron. Her response to her mother was Trevet doesn't have feelings for her that way. They could only be friends. Her mother would disagree, saying Trevet loves her and to give him time, that he'll come around.

"Mom, he cares about me and Aaron, that's all."

"Mama, I see Daddy." Aaron's little voice broke into her thoughts.

Bri smiled at Aaron. "Okay, we see Daddy." Aaron clapped his hands.

Later that day, Bri made reservations for a flight to Atlanta for the next evening. She packed clothes for herself and Aaron. As hard as she tried not to, she felt herself getting excited, and she wanted to see Trevet as much as her son did. Her hands stopped folding clothes. Would he be happy to see her, she wondered? She knew he'd be pleased to see Aaron. Another thought crossed her mind. Maybe Trevet has found someone else. A pain stabbed at her heart as tears filled her eyes.

"Get it together, Bri," she said aloud, blinking back tears.

****

They arrived at her parents' house early evening. Right away, she noticed how her father's health was improving. Aaron ran through the house, looking for Trevet. "Daddy!" he called out.

"Aaron, Daddy's not here yet," Bri told him. "We have to call him, okay?" she said to her son.

Bri looked at her mother with those mother's eyes. "I can see it in your eyes, Bri. Don't read anything into his absence. Trevet has been very busy; I'll call him," her mother told her. "Trevet," she said on the phone, "guess who's looking for you?" Irene handed the phone to Aaron.

"Hi, Daddy," Aaron said on the phone. "Daddy, come see me," he paused. "Okay, Daddy." Aaron handed the phone to Bri.

"Hello, Trevet."

"I'll be right over," he told her. Bri took a deep breath, feeling the excitement in her. It was late, but Aaron waited and refused to go to sleep until he saw the man he called "Daddy".

When the doorbell rang, he ran to the door to open it. "Daddy," he cried.

Trevet picked him up, hugging him tightly.

His eyes met Bri's. "Hello, Bri."

"Hi. You've made a little boy very happy," she replied softly.

"Daddy, we go to play?" Aaron asked with his arm around Trevet's neck.

"Tomorrow; it's too dark now," Trevet promised.

"When is 'morrow, Daddy?" Aaron asked.

"When the sun is in the sky," Trevet answered, chuckling.

Trevet sat down with Aaron on his lap. Her parents had gone to bed a while ago. Bri sat across from Trevet. How she missed him.

"How long are you staying?" he asked.

"I have to get back, but Aaron is going to stay for a while with his grandparents," she stated. Trevet nodded.

He looked down at the boy, who had fallen asleep in his arms. Bri rose to take him.

"I'll take him up," he offered.

Bri sat waiting for Trevet to return. She still wanted him. When she saw him, her heart escalated and that thickness between her thighs had her underwear soaked. Did he want her as badly as she needed him? "Bri, it's good to see you," he said, returning to the room. She stood to her feet.

"You too. Dad says you're working too hard."

He smiled and shrugged. "He's probably right."

Bri went to him and stood in front of him. Trevet looked down at her. Damn, how he missed her. His entire body throbbed with desire. He wanted nothing more than to lose himself between her thighs and make her scream as he brought her to a mind-blowing orgasm. Inwardly calming himself, he decided he better go before he did something he would regret.

Bri stood in front of him, hoping he would just grab her and kiss her. He didn't move. She sighed and gazed into his gray eyes.

"Thanks for coming. Aaron missed you so much," she said. So, did I, she thought to herself.

"He's my son," Trevet said matter-of-factly. "It's late; I better go. Tell Aaron I'll see him tomorrow." He turned to leave.

Bri sighed, feeling dejected. "Okay, Trevet. I'll probably be gone tomorrow."

He turned sharply, "You just got here, Bri."

"I'm going to New York," she stated.

"New York?"

"Yes, there's a gallery that wants to exhibit my paintings. I wasn't sure I would do it, but you helped me decide."

"Me?"

"Goodnight." She turned, leaving him at the door.

Trevet was in the backyard with Aaron and his grandparents. Bri had just returned from her two-week trip to New York, and she wasn't alone. Beside her stood a tall, well-built man. He appeared to be more Bri's age. Trevet felt his heart drop, and pain seared his gut. Bri was holding his hand and smiling up at him. Did he wait too long to claim her as his own? Was he wrong to make her wait because he wasn't sure of himself and her?

"Mama!" Aaron cried and ran to her. Bri released the man's hand, lifted her baby, and hugged him tightly.

"Hello, Baby. Mama missed you so much," she said, hugging him again. Jorge and Irene looked over at Trevet. They both saw the look of disbelief on his face, then disappointment. Bri and her companion came to where they were sitting.

"Hi, Mom and Dad," she said, putting Aaron down and kissing them both. She looked over at Trevet. "Hello, Trevet."

"Brianna," he replied impersonally. Bri frowned. Trevet had never called her by her full name before. She looked into his eyes. He turned away before she could read him. Was he angry, she wondered? "Hello, Sweetie," Irene said with a knowing smile on her face. If Trevet didn't act now, she was sure he would lose Bri because the handsome man that stood beside her seemed besotted with Bri.

"Mom, Dad, Trevet, this is Jason Bourne. I met him in New York," Bri introduced, smiling at him. "Jason is a sculptor; he's been giving me lessons in sculpture." Trevet stood and shook his hand, looking the man directly in his eyes.

"You're from Atlanta?" Trevet asked in a terribly subdued voice.

"No, I'm a New Yorker through and through. I just traveled with Bri because I'm going to have a showing tonight," he said, taking Bri's hand in his and looking at her with affection. "She's offered to show me around."

"Well, Jason, I'd better change if I'm going to show you around Atlanta before we have to go to the exhibit. I won't be long," Bri promised and turned to leave.

She gave Trevet one last glance. He stood aggressively with his hands clasped behind his back. Aaron stood next to him with a similar stance. Bri shook her head and hurried into the house.

"Please sit down, Mr. Bourne. May I get you something to drink?" Irene asked.

"No, I'm fine," Jason said, sitting down beside Jorge.

"You've been sculpting long?" Jorge asked.

"Well, about most of my life, I guess. It's my passion," he said, grinning.

"How did you and Bri meet?" Trevet asked brusquely. Irene smiled. Trevet was jealous. Good, she thought.

Jason told them how he saw her admiring his pieces and introduced himself. She told him how she'd always wanted to sculpt, so he offered her his services.

"Excuse me," Trevet said, going into the house. Bri was coming down the stairs when Trevet entered the house. Trevet stood at the bottom of the stairs as she was coming down. She looked gorgeous with her hair pulled back accentuating her beautiful face. The black strapless jumpsuit hugged her petite waist and hips before the legs flared out to meet the stylish, sexy heels she wore.

"You're wearing that to show him Atlanta?" Trevet asked sullenly.

"Why, what's wrong with this? We're going to the showing right after," Bri said, frowning at him. "I owe you no explanations, Trevet. You've ignored me nearly the entire time I was here and don't feign interest now because I'm with someone else."

"What do you mean 'with'?" he demanded, his voice rising.

"Just that, Trevet," she said as she walked around him and out the patio door.

 Trevet watched through the door as she talked with Jason and her parents. His hands balled into fists, and he grind his teeth. Bri wrapped her stole around her bare shoulders as they took their leave, Irene behind them.

"Trevet," Irene called softly. Trevet turned to her, the sadness on his face visible.

"Go get your woman!" she stated firmly.

"It's too late, Irene," Trevet said, leaving her to get Aaron.

****

Trevet sat in the large overstuffed chair in his robe, wondering what Bri and her new friend were doing. He tried to get some sleep, but all he did was tossed and turned, envisioning Bri in the arms of Jason. His chest hurt and his belly was in knots. He asked himself if he loved Bri, or if he just desired her? He wasn't sure. He did desire her; there was no doubt he wanted her in his bed, but did he love her? Love was something he wasn't sure he knew anything about. He didn't have that in his life, so how could he recognize it? He did know that he didn't like her with another man.

Trevet rose and turned off the TV. The doorbell rang. He looked at the watch on his arm: 12:30 am. He frowned as he opened the door.

"Bri!" he said, surprised to see her. Not waiting to be invited in, she walked past him. She wasn't going to let him turn her away again, not until he knew how she felt about him. Trevet closed the door and turned to look at her. She had changed her clothes; she had on jeans and a T-shirt.

"I love you," she said softly.

Her admission stunned and elated him. His heart swelled with joy. Trevet swept her off her feet, carrying her to his bedroom. If he never made love to her again, he was going to tonight. He gently put her on the bed and lay beside her. He didn't hesitate; he pressed his lips to hers, kissing her with the passion of a drowning man. Bri wrapped her arms around his neck and held him to her. She pulled her mouth from his, pushing his robe from his shoulders as her lips sought his chest.

"Bri," Trevet said, panting. "Please, Trevet, don't send me away. I want you," she pleaded. Trevet looked into her eyes. She rolled away and removed her clothing quickly. "Make love to me, Trevet." Trevet's mouth was on her. Bri sighed as his lips trailed down her body and feasted on her breasts. He shifted and entered her.

"Yesss," she moaned, feeling him inside her. She wanted him, and she'd thought of nothing else the whole time she was in New York. She decided she would see him and make love to him.

"I love you," she murmured, loving the connection to him again.

Her hands roamed all over his body. Trevet pulled out of her; she protested.

"Ride me, Bri," he said huskily. She straddled him and sank down on him. Her breath caught in her chest at the feeling of him inside her. She moved up and down on him slowly, savoring his manhood inside her. His hands on her breasts kneaded them softly. He pulled her body down to him and took them into his mouth, sucking her nipples. Bri moaned softly, loving his mouth on her. Trevet rolled her to her back, still connected. Her legs went up around his waist as he moved in and out of her fiery wetness. Her eyes gazed at this handsome face. She loved him and would always love him, even though she realized he didn't love her. She would definitely love him tonight. Their eyes met. His gray eyes penetrated her soul and pulled at her heart. Bri gasped; her orgasm was there. Her walls contracted around his hardness, and her body moved with each shiver that she was giving him.

"Bri," he said breathlessly. He felt her walls pull at him, causing him to sink deeper. He lifted her hips and sank into her deeper than he ever had. Trevet moved inside her with a lack of restraint, not wanting this moment ever to end.

"Trevet," Bri cried and let the orgasm consume her as he joined her in perfect sensual bliss. They lay together, each one quiet.

"This shouldn't have happened, Bri," Trevet said, breaking the silence.

Bri leaned up on her elbows and looked into his face. His eyes were closed, and anguish was on his face. Tears filled her eyes. She got out of the bed, dressed, and left.

Trevet arrived at Irene and Jorge's the next morning. He always had breakfast with Aaron, but he wanted to see Bri. He needed to explain to her why he said what he did last night. He had to make her understand.

"Good Morning," Trevet greeted everyone, lifting Aaron.

"Good Morning, Son," Jorge said. Trevet sat at the table. He glanced toward the stairs, expecting Bri to come down any minute.

"Daddy, Mama go bye-bye," Aaron informed Trevet.

Surprise registered on Trevet's face. He looked at Irene and Jorge.

"Trevet Harrison, what are you waiting for?" Irene asked him.

"I don't know what you mean," he stated.

"Of course you do, Son," Jorge said.

"You love Bri," Irene said. "So why are you not going after her?"

"I'm not sure she's ready for us to be together. Trevet became alarmed. "Is she seeing that Jason?" he asked.

Irene shrugged. "It's possible. She talked about him a lot."

"Did she say she was seeing him?" he asked a little gruffly.

"To be honest, Son, I don't know. She said she may go back to New York after she finished her jobs in Virginia," Irene said, stretching the truth a little.

Jorge smiled. He knew Irene was stretching the truth; all Bri talked about was Trevet.

"I'm going to Virginia," he announced to Irene. Irene and Jorge smiled.

"Don't worry about Aaron. He'll be okay."

Chapter Nine

Trevet stood nervously outside of Bri's condo, praying he wasn't too late to claim his woman. He hadn't wasted any time flying to Virginia to see her. He wanted her back in Atlanta; she could do her painting there. He remembered reading an article about her exhibition in New York where she received rave reviews for several of her pieces. Some of her cultural paintings are placed in the African American art museums in New York and Georgia. He was immensely proud of her. Somehow, he had to convince her to stay in Atlanta. Although he cherished his time with Aaron, he missed the time they spent together with the little boy. Did he wait too long to claim her, he again wondered? He knew she wanted him, but at the time, he thought it would be best that they slow things down. At least that's what he thought. Irene was right. He was the one that was scared.

Trevet took a deep breath and rang the doorbell. The door opened. "Yes?" a good-looking man at the door replied, dressed in a bathrobe that was partially open to his waist. Trevet looked at the medium height man with disdain. His heart fell to his feet. He was too late, he thought.

"Can I help you?" the other man asked. Trevet had to contain himself from punching him in the face just for being at her house.

"Is Bri here?" he asked, holding a tight rein on his temper.

"Yes, she is. Who should I say is calling?" he replied politely.

"Who is it, Kiev?" Bri called from inside the house.

The man turned, "I have no idea."

"Well, send them away. I want to get done."

Kiev turned back to Trevet. "I'm sorry; she's busy. Stop..."

Trevet pushed him out the way, crossing the threshold. "Bri!" he called loudly through the house.

Bri came out of her studio in the back of the house. She had on jeans and a T-shirt, her hair loosely pulled back, paint smudges on her cheek and chin, and a paintbrush in her hand. Kiev looked at Trevet with a raised brow.

"Trevet," she said, surprised then concerned. "What's wrong? Is Aaron okay?"

"He's fine," Trevet said gruffly. "What's going on?"

Ignoring his question, Bri gave a sigh of relief. "You scared me."

"You didn't answer my question, Brianna." Bri's brow puckered, now showing her growing anger. "You're right, Trevet. I'm busy."

After her initial surprise and concern, she thought it terribly rude of Trevet to barge into her home. How dare he demand answers from her. He's the one who ignored her for months, now here he is asking what she was doing.

"Kiev, we can finish tomorrow," she told him.

"You sure, Bri? I mean—I can..." Trevet turned and scowled at him.

"Get lost, Kiev," Trevet said, interrupting him. He smugly walked to Bri and kissed each of her cheeks. "If you say so."

Bri silently glared at Trevet.

Kiev quickly gathered his things and was gone. Bri turned and went into her studio. Trevet followed. He leaned against the doorjamb, watching Bri cleanup.

"Who was that?" Trevet repeated the question.

Bri turned. "Who do you think he was?"

"Your lover," he stated firmly.

"Not that I owe you any explanation, Trevet, but he's my model," she replied, moving around and cleaning.

"Is that all?" he asked tersely. Bri stopped what she was doing and faced an angry Trevet. If she didn't know any better, she would think he was jealous. How ridiculous is that she thought.

"I'm not answering any outlandish questions from you," she declared stubbornly.

Trevet suddenly moved to her and grabbed her, startling her. Her mind flashed back to Tyrone. She remembered the look on his face just before he would punch her in the face, but she was not about to let history repeat itself.

She jerked away from him. "I will not be beaten again," she told him fiercely, staring him squarely in his eyes.

"Beat you! I would never hurt you, Bri," he said, dropping his hands.

She looked at him and knew he would never hurt her. "Why are you here, Trevet?" she asked.

"Are you sleeping with him?"

Bri turned, ignoring him.

"You will answer me!" he yelled.

Bri jumped. "He's gay. He'd rather have you. Why are you here, Trevet?" she countered. "When I was at my parents, you barely had two words for me. So why are you here now?"

Trevet exhaled, gradually calming down.

"Answer me, Trevet," she demanded.

"I came to get you," he stated matter-of-factly. Bri frowned.

"Why?" She stopped to look at him.

"Because, you love me," he stated arrogantly.

"Not anymore," she said. Bri left the room and went up the stairs. A look of astonishment was on his face. Trevet couldn't believe she would just leave him standing there as if he weren't there. He followed her up the stairs. When he entered her bedroom, she had just removed her clothes.

"You're just going to dismiss me, just like that?"

"Yep," she said and went to get in the shower.

Trevet looked at the door she just went into, confusion on his face. He followed her. His breath caught in his chest at the sight of her nude body. He could feel his body heating up as he observed her glistening body while water cascaded over it. He wanted her. No, he needed her. He wanted to go to her, wanted to feel her wet body pressed to his. He was staring at her so intently, he didn't notice the shower had stopped. She stood naked, watching him.

Bri watched the emotions on his face. He wanted her, she recognized. How many nights did she want him? How many nights did she cry because of his rejection? However, he'd pushed her away. Well, she had her pride. She would not give into her body's demands. She would not beg him to love her. Wrapping a towel around her body, she walked around him and out of the bathroom. Trevet knew he had to regain his composure.

He entered the dimly lit bedroom. Bri stood on the balcony looking out at the ocean. The heavy, full moon gave light to her small, towel-wrapped frame as she leaned against the rail. Beside her was a covered painting on an easel. "I love her," he whispered. The realization stunned him, and his heart swelled with happiness.

"Bri," he said softly. She turned to him. The moonlight reflected the tears that glistened on her face. She turned away. Trevet walked up behind her and placed his hands on her shoulders. She moved away from him.

"Don't do this to me, Trevet," she said, her voice choking on her tears.

"Bri, please," he said softly. "Don't push me away now. I need you in my life."

She turned sharply, now angry.

"When did you decide that, Trevet?" she asked him.

"I've always needed you; it was just happening too fast. We needed to slow what was building between us. You needed to have time to know me, just as I needed to know you, don't you …"?

"Shut up, Trevet!" she yelled at him. "I didn't need time; you needed time. I knew I wanted you even before the night we made love, so please stop with this self-righteous act."

Trevet stood stunned; but in his heart, he knew she was right. He was the one who wanted to slow things down.

She went to him, looking directly into his eyes. Her eyes were red from crying. "Bri, I thought it was best. We hadn't known each other long enough to fall into a relationship.

"So you regret that we made love?" she asked. "No," she said, covering her ears. "I couldn't bear it if I thought you regretted it."

Trevet pulled her hands from her ears. "I don't regret it, Bri. Please understand. We were just moving too fast. I didn't know what I felt. All I knew was that I wanted more than just great sex."

"Why didn't you say that? I felt rejected by you."

"That was not my intention. I wanted you to be sure we had more in common than the fact that we make love so well together." Trevet dropped his head. "I can't lose you, Bri," he said softly.

His head rose, and he looked at her. "I'm sorry, Bri. Am I too late?"

She stepped closer to him and laid her head on his chest. Trevet breathed a sigh of relief and held her close. Her arms went around his waist.

Bri exhaled. I love him so much, she thought. Her head rose. Rising up on her toes, she pressed her lips to his. Trevet held her face between his hands, deepening the kiss. Damn, he missed her and that perfect mouth. Bri let the towel fall from her body. She pressed closer to him, craving the feel of his body against hers. She broke the kiss. Her heart pounded in her chest; she wanted him. She tore at his shirt. Her hands finally made contact with his hot skin, and his muscles contracted under her touch. Her mouth moved boldly on his chest. She stepped back to look up at him with pent-up passion clearly in her eyes. Her hands fumbled with the buckle of his belt. Trevet's hand covered hers. She stopped and looked at him.

"I want you, Trevet. Please don't reject me again."

Quickly he removed his pants. His manhood stood proudly thick and long before her. She reached and took his throbbing shaft in her small hands, gently stroking him. Trevet groaned, and his eyes closed as he savored the feel of her little hands on him. Her lips pressed kisses on his chest and lowered as she still stroked him. Bri dropped to her knees and lovingly kissed the tip of his throbbing manhood. Her tongue licked up the length of him before taking him into her mouth. Trevet groaned loudly as she loved him with her mouth. He felt a weakness in his legs. He lifted her from her knees, guided her legs around his waist, and quickly entered her as her arms wrapped around his neck.

Bri cried out his name when he entered her. Her head fell back, and her eyes drifted shut. Her breathing was cumbersome and rapid, as was Trevet's. He effortlessly walked their joined bodies to the bed. Gently, he put her down on the bed. She looked up into his steel colored eyes. Their lips met hungrily. Trevet moved inside her slow at first but quickened the pace after her first orgasm, hearing her cry his name in his ear. His hands immobilized her hips, wanting to take what she was giving him. He stroked her until she was sure she would burst into flames. Together they strove toward the pinnacle of pure bliss. She felt him sink deeper into her, her body welcoming him. She held on to him tightly and lost all sense of reason, except for the pleasure that was invading all her senses. She pulsated even stronger around Trevet's manhood as he drove deep into her welcoming body. Bri cried his name repeatedly. Trevet took her mouth wildly, and her hands clawed at his back. "Trevet, please," she moaned.

"Not yet, Baby," he said in her ear and rolled to his back their bodies still attached. He held her hips and controlled the pace of their lovemaking. He lifted her so just the tip of his throbbing manhood was inside her. Her head fell back when he slowly slid her back down on him, only to lift her again. He held her suspended above him, her wet opening just resting on him. He pushed into her, rotating and pulling just enough from her walls to feel warm juices coating his hardened manhood.

"Please," she moaned. Slowly he gave her every inch of him until he was fully inside her. He could feel the rhythmic pull of her orgasm, and yet he knew she had more. He stroked her very soul. He reached up and clasped her face in his hands while his hips still pushed up inside her. He demanded she focus on this moment. "Bri," he said, panting and holding a tight rein on his pleasure.

74

Her eyes opened. "I love you. I would never hurt you. I'll protect you with my life." His eyes closed for a brief second. He was losing control; the need for him to come was consuming him. Her walls tightened around him, causing his manhood to expand. He rolled her onto her back. She cried his name and pleaded for a sweet release. Trevet rose up on his hands, sinking deeper into her moist cavern. Her head tilted back, exposing her neck. "Trevet, please," she moaned.

"Now, baby," he moaned into her ear, and he stroked the dormant fires consuming them both. Trevet never felt anything as mind blowing as he did at this moment. She pushed her hips to meet him with wild abandonment. Her legs went around his waist, and he reared up thrusting inside, taking her to an ecstasy they both desperately needed. Their cries echoed off the walls. Trevet rolled from on top of her, closing his arms around her. They lay quietly, both unsure if they could speak as they basked in the aftermath of their love.

"I love you, Trevet," she said softly. He kissed the top of her head.

"Bri, don't ever leave me," he said softly.

"I love you, Trevet. I'll never leave you."

Bri awoke alone and looked around the semi-dark room. Trevet stood on the balcony. The sun was just beginning to rise; its rays reflected its golden hues on the bay. Trevet stood looking at the portrait. Bri rose, wrapped the sheet around her, and joined him. He looked over at her and smiled.

"It's beautiful," he said. The portrait was of him and Aaron while he read to him. The love in Trevet's eyes was captured as he looked down at Aaron, and the adoration was in Aaron's eyes as he looked up at him. Trevet pulled her close to him as they silently observed the painting. His heart swelled with love and pride. He had a family, and he felt blessed, for he loved Bri and Aaron with all his heart. He took her hand and led her to the bed. Bri climbed on the bed and sat in the middle. Trevet left her and went downstairs. A minute later, he returned and stood at the foot of the bed. Bri frowned.

"Bri, are you coming back to Atlanta?" Trevet asked.

"Yes."

"Are you finished with the commissions?"

"No, I have to finish Kiev."

"How much time do you need?"

"I could finish today, with no interruptions," she smiled. "Why are you asking so many questions?"

He joined her on the bed, sitting beside her. Bri turned her head to look at him. He pushed the sheet she was wrapped in from her back. Soft kisses journeyed down her spine.

"Trevet," she said breathlessly. He continued kissing her spine. Bri pulled away from him and rose up on her knees. Trevet pulled her on top of him. His hands cupped her butt, and he ground against her. "Trevet, what are you doing?" He kissed her.

"I'm going to make love to my fiancée," he stated. Bri leaned up and looked at him, her eyes wide and mouth opened. Trevet laughed. He rolled her onto her back; still she stared up at him in astonishment. Trevet became serious.

"Bri, I never knew what it was like to love someone, the way I love you. I had no family except for your Mother and Father. I love Aaron as if he were my own son; you and Aaron are my life, and I want us to be a family. I promise to love you and Aaron with all my heart, protect you from harm, and cherish you. Bri Cleyvon, will you and Aaron marry me?"

Bri was so choked up, she couldn't speak.

He raised his hand, and on his pinky, was a five carat diamond ring. "Marry me, Bri. I promise to make you happy." Tears rolled down the side of her face.

"I love you," she said tearfully. Trevet lifted her hand and put the ring on her finger. He kissed her mouth.

"So, you didn't answer my question."

"Yes, Trevet, I'll be proud to be your wife. Now shut up and make love to me."

Chapter Ten

One year later

Bri watched her son running around the playground as she sketched him and the other children while they played. It was a beautiful spring day. The azure sky was dotted with white cotton ball clouds. Bri took a deep breath.

"Mama," Aaron called, "look at me," as he hung from the monkey bars. She hated seeing when he does that. Trevet taught him to hang upside down, swinging by his legs. "That's really good, baby, but be careful, Aaron."

After the large, lavish wedding her mother and father insisted she have, Trevet formally adopted Aaron, who is now christened as Jorge Aaron Harrison. Bri never thought she could be as happy as she is now. Her father was getting better with his prostate cancer; her mother was happy to fuss over him. She and Trevet built their dream home, and he surprised her by having an art studio added when the house was constructed. She had another successful exhibit in Atlanta, with rave reviews, where she displayed the painting she named *"Adoration."* The generous offers she received for that particular picture were staggering, but Trevet informed them that particular painting was not for sale. She had a family of her own and was blessed that her life had taken such a positive turn.

"Mama look," Aaron called out. He was climbing up the slide, laying on his belly and sliding down. "That's good, Aaron," she said, smiling.

"Hello, Bri," a voice said behind her.

She turned. "Tyrone!" she said stunned and coming to her feet.

"How are you?" he said.

"What do you want? You are not to be around us."

Bri rushed away, her heart pounding in her chest.

"You used to care about me, Bri," Tyrone said, acting as if his feelings were hurt.

"What is it that you want?" she repeated.

Tyrone sneered at her. "You always were a snob, Bri. What do you think I want? The only thing you were ever good for: money."

She frowned at him. "You had $100,000, and it's gone already?!" she said incredulously.

"Aaron!" she called. "Come on!"

"Okay, Mama!" he answered as he jumped from the swing and ran to her. When he reached her, she took his hand and walked away from Tyrone. Bri took in her surroundings. There were many people at the park, and he wouldn't dare try anything now. She pressed the button to unlock the car. She opened the door and put Aaron in, locking the door. "Lock yourself in the seat, Aaron."

Going to the driver side, she saw Tyrone approaching them. She reached for the door handle with trembling hands. She was frightened. All she knew was she had to get away from Tyrone. Bri pulled open the door.

Tyrone grabbed her arm, turning her around. "Bitch, don't ignore me. I need money!" he said in her face. "I don't have any money," she lied.

"Oh yeah, you married that lawyer; I know he's loaded." Get in the car, Bri," he said through clenched teeth.

"Help me," she screamed loudly.

"Shut up!" Tyrone said, slapping her hard across her face.

Aaron started crying in the back seat. Bri was dazed but was determined not to get in the car with him. She opened her mouth to scream again. He reached into his pants and pulled out a gun, pressing it to her side. People were starting to notice her struggling. Tyrone looked over his shoulder,

"Get in the car, Bri - now!" Bri pulled open the door and slid inside.

She looked at Aaron, whose eyes were wide with fear. "Mama, that man hit you," he cried.

"It's okay, sweetie," she said, wiping the blood from her mouth.

"Give me the keys, Bri," Tyrone yelled.

"No!" she screamed at him. He lifted the gun and pointed it at Aaron. Bri's heart froze.

"I swear I'll blow his brains out," he warned, cocking the gun.

Bri quickly threw the keys at him. Her fist beat on the window. "Help me!" she screamed. "Please help me; somebody help me."

"Shut up!" he yelled and hit her in the back of her head with the butt of the gun, dazing her. Aaron was screaming in the back seat. Unhooking himself, he jumped on Tyrone's head and hit him with his little fist, shouting, "Don't hit my Mama! Don't hit my Mama!"

Tyrone pushed Aaron off him. Bri reached over and dug her nails into his face. Tyrone hit her again with the blunt end of his gun, causing blood to drip down the side of her face. A man ran and approached the car. Tyrone pointed his gun at the man.

"Don't die for this bitch," he shouted at the man. Bri slumped against the door, dazed, as Aaron screamed her name at the top of his lungs. Tyrone started the car and sped off. The man quickly dialed 911.

"Bri, Aaron!" Trevet called as he came through the door. Coming home to his family was always the best time of his day. It was remarkable how his once ordinary life had changed when Bri and Aaron came into his life. He smiled. He felt such pride when he adopted Aaron, making him his son and giving him his name. From the first time he called him Mama, he was lost. He never thought he could love two people as much as he loved his wife and son. He now knows what family means.

"Hey, Dad's home!" Trevet called again. He went to the upstairs of their new home. Bri did a superb job in making this house a home. He went to his bedroom; he frowned and looked at his watch. Five o'clock.

"They should have been home by now," he said aloud. The phone rang. He smiled. They're late, he thought.

"Hello."

"Son," Jorge said.

"Yes, sir."

"I need you to get over here right away." Trevet felt a lump form in his belly.

"What's wrong, Dad."

"Son, just get here, please."

"Bri and …" "Just get over here, Tre, please."

"I'll be right there," he said and hung up the phone.

Jorge Cleyvon paced the floor. Irene stood waiting for Trevet, tears streaming down her face. When the police alerted him of the abduction of his daughter and grandson, he knew he had to get to Trevet before they did. Jorge looked over at his wife; she was wringing her hands and crying.

"Mother, you must stop. I need to break this to him gently."

"Jorge, he's going to know something is wrong with the police outside," she said, looking out the window, "and who alerted the media?"

"Damn," Jorge swore as he looked out the window.

"He's here," Irene told her husband.

Trevet frowned when he saw the many police cruisers parked in his in-laws' yard. Parking, he got out of the car and was instantly bombarded by the media.

"What's going on?" he asked his father-in-law.

The police pushed the media back. Jorge stood in the door,

"Get them off my property!" he yelled.

Trevet walked past him into the house. "Mom," he said, "what's wrong?"

"Sit down, Son," Jorge told him.

"Dad, what's going on?" He glanced from one to the other.

"Son, Bri and Aaron have been abducted," he stated directly.

The knots that formed in Trevet's stomach grew larger. Trevet sprung to his feet. Jorge looked at the large man. If Trevet lost control, it would be difficult to restrain him. Trevet took a shaky breath, his large hands balling into fists.

"Dad, where is my family?" he asked calmly.

Three officers had entered the house and stood by the door. T

Trevet looked over at Irene. "Mom, please."

Tears filled his eyes. Irene went to him and took his hands in hers.

"Trevet," Jorge said, taking a deep breath. "Tyrone has abducted Bri and your son at gunpoint."

82

Trevet lifted his mother-in-law's hands and softly kissed them. Turning from her, he headed for the door. "Son, where are you going?" Jorge asked frantically.

"I'm going to get my family," he said calmly.

"Trevet, we don't know where they are. The police..."

"Dad, I can't sit here and wait for the police when my family is in danger. I promised Bri I would protect her and our son with my life. I'm going to find my family," he ground out.

"Trevet, honey, please wait. We need more information about the situation," Irene tried to convince him. "Mom, he has my family!" he shouted and went to the door.

The police barred his way. Trevet looked at them; his gray eyes were like black coals.

"I'm going to say this once...Move!"

Irene rushed over and stood in front of the police. She knew he wouldn't hurt her, but she was not sure about the men that were standing in front of the door. Jorge went to him and placed his hand on his back. "Son, please. You can't go out half-cocked. He's armed, and we have to be careful," he replied calmly. Trevet turned to Jorge. He was trembling with pent-up rage. "That's my family!" he roared so loud, the media outside quieted. Trevet looked at Jorge helplessly. "Dad, please," he said and lowered his head, sobbing.

"God, please protect my family until I can find them," he prayed. Irene went to her husband, crying openly now.

"Come on, Son. We must keep the faith. Come sit, so we can formulate a plan. The detective is here to tell us all he knows."

Trevet listened, his body tense with constrained rage. "We have an Amber Alert out on your wife's car and your son Aaron. Mr. Harrison, right now we have no hits, but we are optimistic."

"How long ago did this happen, Captain," Trevet asked shakily.

"The abduction was reported about one o'clock this afternoon," the detective replied.

"Tell me everything," Trevet demanded.

"The witness said he saw Tyrone slap your wife and then pushed her into the car. They argued for a minute. The witness then observed the man pointing a gun at your son; that's when she threw something at him. Your son tried to help his mother. When Tyrone slapped her again, that little fellow jumped on him from the back seat. He pushed the boy to the back of the car, and that's when she attacked Tyrone. He had hit her with the gun a couple of times before she passed out. The witness said he approached the car, but Tyrone pointed the gun at him, threatening to shoot him. That's when he called 911."

The pain that was raging though his heart was his undoing. "I can't sit. I need to do something." His hulking frame paced the floor like a caged animal. "He put his hands on my family," Trevet kept muttering to himself.

****

Tyrone brought Bri and Aaron to some seedy motel on the outskirts of Atlanta. He grabbed Aaron by the arm, pulling him roughly with them.

"Get your purse, and you better hope you have some cash in it. If you scream, I swear I'll put a cap in this brat," he threatened, shaking Aaron like a rag doll.

He handed her the motel room key. Bri pushed the door open. Tyrone pushed her into the room and dragged Aaron behind, pushing him into her. Bri held Aaron on her lap, trying to calm him down. She watched as deranged Tyrone paced the floor, talking to himself.

"Call my husband. He'll give you money," she said after a few minutes.

Tyrone stopped pacing and glared at her evilly. "Somebody better," he sneered. "Shut that damn kid up!" he yelled.

"Shh... Shh... Aaron, Daddy's coming," she whispered. Bri dug in the purse, pulled out her phone, and held it out to him. "Call my husband. He'll..."

"Damn right he will if he wants you and the brat back." Bri held Aaron tightly in her arms.

"Daddy's coming, Baby," she cooed.

"Stop making a punk out of that kid!" he yelled, snatching the screaming Aaron by his arm from her lap. Bri jumped up. "Don't touch my son, you bastard. I'll kill you if you hurt him!" she screamed.

Tyrone backhanded Aaron across the face; he went flying across the room. "Shut up, kid!"

Leaping at him, Bri clawed his face and swung at him with all her might. Surprised by her attack and finding it difficult to get her off him, he managed to push her down on the bed and lay on her.

"Oh, so you got a little hellion in you," he chuckled, holding her down.

"How about I screw you like I used to, little hellcat?"

Bri's strength renewed. Getting her hand free, she dug her nails deep into his face.

"Bitch," Tyrone cried, rolling off her. Bri tried to scramble off the bed. Tyrone recovered and dragged her from the bed to the floor. Bri turned to her back and kicked him as hard as she could in his chest, causing him to lose his grip on her. He punched her in the face, but Bri didn't stop fighting. She fought with everything she had. Aaron screamed in the background, cowering in the corner of the room. Tyrone rolled from her, panting for breath. Bri scrambled to her feet, going to Aaron. He caught her arm, pulled her back to him, and crashed his fist into her face. She fell at his feet and curled into a ball as he kicked her in the back. She learned that protective move when she carried Aaron. After the third kick, Bri grabbed his leg, sank her teeth into him as hard as she could, and held on for dear life. Tyrone screamed out and began punching her in the head until she released his leg. Aaron crawled to his semi-conscious mother, screaming her name.

"Shut up, kid!" he yelled at Aaron while gasping for breath.

Tyrone picked up her purse, rummaging through it. He found one hundred dollars along with every platinum and gold card that's offered. This was not going as he had planned. He didn't expect the scary bitch to fight back. He knew he had to get out of there before management alerted the police. After that bitch had attacked him, making all that noise, he was sure others heard her screams with these paper-thin walls. He glared down at his unconscious ex-wife. He should have held out for more money when they asked him to sign over his parental rights. The one hundred thousand they gave him was gone within a few months. He glared over at her son screaming her name at the top of his lungs. He had a mind to take the brat with him and ask for a ransom, but common sense told him that he would make things worse for himself if he kidnapped the boy and they found him. He just better cut his losses and hightail it out of here.

Chapter Eleven

They kept the television on, all watching for the amber alert caption to move across the bottom of the screen. Trevet sat staring at the TV and praying for word about his family.

"Dad, I can't take this waiting. Are the police even looking?"

"I know this is killing you slowly, Son, but we have to have patience," Jorge replied.

"Patience! My wife and son are out there with that lunatic. I just…" Trevet shouted, came to his feet, and paced back and forth.

"Breaking News," the commentator on the television screen said. "It is reported that Tyrone Grant was spotted at the Peachtree ATM. We're told the police have apprehended him and taken him into custody; no word on Brianna Harrison or her son."

Trevet didn't hesitate. He dashed from the house, jumped into his car, and headed for the police station. Trevet arrived at the police station as if the hounds of hell were behind him. Tyrone was handcuffed in the interrogation room. The captain of the police allowed Trevet to listen to see if his family's whereabouts would be revealed by Tyrone.

"Where are Bri and her son?" the detective demanded.

Tyrone laughed. "See what that bitch did to my face. She deserves what she got. I ain't talking no more unless you givin' me a deal."

"Look, Grant, you are in no position to bargain for anything. Where are Bri and her son?" the detective yelled, leaning on the table in Tyrone's face.

"I want a lawyer," Tyrone stated smugly. He leaned back in the chair he sat on and put his feet on the table. The detective glared at him, knocking his feet to the floor.

Tyrone laughed.

"Captain, please let me in there. That's my family—if he's killed…" Trevet choked on the words "them…"

"Okay, five minutes," the captain agreed.

Trevet walked in the room. He immediately sensed the fear in Tyrone.

"Grant, where's my family?" Trevet said ominously. Tyrone looked at Trevet and literally shook with fear of him. This big hulk of a man could kill him with one blow. Despite his fear, Tyrone couldn't help but make a proposition.

"How much is it worth?" he grinned.

"You're not going to need money, where you're going," Trevet retorted.

Tyrone shrugged. "Yeah, maybe not, but I got my memories of screwing her. She begged for more. You really made a little whore out of her. She used to be so cold," he chuckled.

Trevet leaped across the table at Tyrone. The detectives in the room turned their backs for a few minutes before they pulled Trevet off him. He had pummeled Grant senseless; he lay unconscious in the corner of the room. A knock on the door stopped Trevet from trying to further beat him.

"Mr. Harrison, you need to hear this. Come with me."

Trevet forgot about Tyrone and left the room.

"There's this kid looking for his Daddy cause his Mama won't wake up. We think it's your son." "Aaron," Trevet said into the phone.

"Daddy," he sobbed. "Mama won't wake up, Daddy. Come and get us. Mama said you were coming." "I'm coming. Tell me about Mama."

"Mama's face is hurt. She has lots of hurts. That man hurt Mama," he cried. "She won't wake up." "Aaron, shake Mama hard as you can."

"Mama, Mama," he screamed. "Daddy, she won't wake up."

"We got the address," the captain told him. "Let's go."

"Stay with Mama, Son. I'm coming."

The police cruiser pulled in front of the dilapidated motel where his family was held. Trevet jumped from the car going into the office.

"A woman and a little boy, what room?"

"116" the woman said. Trevet raced up the pavement.

"Aaron!" he called. "Daddy!"

"Open the door, Son."

"You said never leave Mama."

"I'm here now, Son. Open the door, so I can help your Mama."

The door opened slowly. Trevet breathed a sigh of relief, scooped up his son, and went to Bri. She lay motionless on the floor, her face covered in blood.

"My God, Bri," Trevet said, looking at her. The paramedic was behind him.

"Sir, let me check her." Trevet ignored him.

"Bri!" he yelled. "Baby, please." She lay still.

"Shake her hard, Daddy," Aaron told his father.

"I'm sorry, Bri," Trevet said. He shook her hard.

She awoke, swinging. "Bri, Bri, it's me," he said, catching her arms and holding them.

"Tre, Tre," she cried and fell into his arms. She saw Aaron and held him tightly.

"Ma'am, we need to check you out," the paramedic insisted. "I'm fine," she said.

"Baby, let them check you out," Trevet told her. "Ma'am, your nose is broken, and you may have a slight concussion. We have to get you to the hospital."

"No, Tre," she said, frowning. "I don't need..."

"Baby, shh... you have to."

"Check my son" Trevet ordered. The paramedic checked Aaron. "A few bruises but he's fine."

While Bri was examined, Jorge and Irene arrived at the hospital. "Oh, Baby, I'm so sorry," her mother said, holding her hand. Bri's right eye was swollen shut, her lips cut and swollen, and her broken nose had tape across it.

"I feel better than I look, Mom," she said. Her father took her hand and kissed it. Bri looked over at Trevet. He sat quietly in the chair, holding a sleeping Aaron. Jorge went to stand beside him while his wife fussed over their daughter.

"Son," Jorge said, "let it go."

Trevet looked up at Jorge. "I can't."

"Trevet, they're safe now," he said, rubbing his grandson's head.

"I know, Dad, but it's something Grant said that bothers me," Trevet rose, handing Aaron to him.

"I can't talk about this now." He left the room. Bri frowned.

"Trevet's been so quiet since we've come to the hospital." She knew her husband; something was bothering him.

"Dad?" she questioned.

"I'll talk to him," her mother said, following Trevet out the door.

Trevet was sitting in the family waiting room, holding his head in his hands. Irene sat beside him. "Tre," she said softly, "let's talk."

"Mom, I can't," he murmured.

"Do you love my daughter?" Irene asked. Trevet sat up and looked his mother-in-law in her eyes. "With all my heart."

"Talk to her, Tre. She's been through something horrible. She needs you and your love."

Trevet put his arm around her.

"Thank you," he said softly.

"We'll take Aaron home with us; you stay with your wife."

Chapter Twelve

Two months later

She looked out the window of her studio. It was a gloomy day or was it just her mood? Trevet had been very distant with her since that thing with Tyrone. He spent more and more time away from home, only giving his time to Aaron. His working hours got longer and mornings earlier. The weekends were no better. He and Aaron would be gone before she woke up in the mornings. Something was wrong. She tried being intimate with him, but he would always say he was too tired. That's the way it's been, and she was getting damned tired of it.

Her brow creased. "Is he having an affair?" she asked aloud. She shook her head; she wouldn't believe that. Not Trevet. Well, Mr. Harrison, she decided tonight they would have it out for the last time. Bri called her mother to help develop her plan. Bri glanced at the clock: six p.m. Trevet should be home soon. Although he worked late, he always came home before Aaron's bedtime then would return to his office. He would be in for a surprise tonight. Tonight will be a romantic dinner for them, with all the trimmings.

The dining room table was elegantly set with scented candlelight intricately arranged to illuminate the room. Soft romantic music filled the air, and she was pleased with the way her backless black dress hugged her curves. Her loose hair brushed her shoulders in soft curls. He should be walking through that door any minute. She heard the door open. Her heart pounded. She stood when she saw him in the archway of the dining room.

"Hello, Tre," she said softly.

Trevet looked at Bri and around the room. I can't do this, he thought to himself, turning away from her. "Where's Aaron?" he asked grimly.

"Mom's."

"Why?" His expression was hard and bitter.

"I thought we needed time alone, Trevet, don't you?"

"No," he said gruffly, picking up the mail from the side table and looking through it.

"I barely see you anymore. You don't talk to me, let alone touch me. What have I done?" she asked pleadingly.

He turned from her. Bri frowned and stared at his back. Sickening thoughts of him with another woman raced through her mind. The air was suddenly thick with animosity cloaking the room. How stupid was she? "Damn you, you're having an affair," she accused.

He quietly turned to walk out of the room. Bri felt like her throat was closing. Heavy hearted, burning tears slipped from her eyes.

"Trevet, you can't even look at me. Do you love her?" she choked.

Silence. Bri lowered her head, the fight leaving her. "This has been going on for two months now. Okay, Trevet, you win, and I'm gone." Bri strode further back into the dining room, blowing out the many candles she had lit. The tears dropped from her eyes; angrily she swiped at them. Trevet turned, watching her. He loved her, but he just couldn't deal with what Tyrone had said to him. He had raped her, and she never said anything to him. He didn't want to lose her, but he couldn't erase the vision from his head of Bri withering beneath Grant.

"Bri," he said softly.

She turned to look at him. "How could you, Trevet? I would never allow another man to touch me," she screamed.

"Then you lie, Bri," he said angrily.

Bri blistered indignantly. "Lie? I have never lied to you."

Trevet chuckled mirthlessly. "No, that is true; you just never admitted it."

"What are you talking about? Admit what?"

"Just tell me, Bri!" he demanded.

Tired of this back and forth with Trevet, Bri replied disheartened, "You know what Trevet? I'm not doing this with you. I have nothing to admit."

She walked past him, pausing to look up at him with sadness in her eyes. "Go get comfort from your lover," she sneered, moving away from him.

He grabbed her arm. "I want you to tell me about Tyrone."

"Tyrone? What are you talking about?"

"Just tell me, Bri!" he yelled. "Tell you what, Trevet? He attacked me; I fought back. That's all." "What else?" He grabbed her arm. She pulled away from him. "There's nothing else!" Bri walked past him and went up the stairs to their bedroom. She pulled out her suitcase and began putting things into it. Trevet stood in the doorway.

"What are you doing?" he asked.

"Making room for your girlfriend," she said sarcastically.

"You're not going anywhere," he stated firmly.

Bri stopped and looked at him. "Watch me," she said and began packing another suitcase.

"You promised you'd never leave me," he replied, desperation in his tone.

"I lied," she said sarcastically. Ignoring him, Bri pulled off her dress and slipped on underwear, jeans, and T-shirt. She brushed her hair and pulled it back into a ponytail. She picked up her suitcases and started for the door. Trevet blocked her way.

"Move, Trevet."

"I won't allow you to leave me, Bri," Trevet growled at her.

"What difference does it make, Trevet? You act like I'm not here anyway," she said sharply.

"That's not true."

"Whatever, Trevet," she said, pushing past him.

Trevet grabbed her around her waist and picked her up to carry her back to the bedroom with her bags still in her hands.

Bri dropped the bags. "Put me down, you big ox!" she raged at him.

Trevet took her back to their bedroom, put her down and locked the door. He leaned against the door. "Bri, you can't leave me," he said earnestly, moving closer to her.

"Do you honestly think, Trevet, I am going to share you?"

"I'm not having an affair, Bri."

"Really? Well then, Trevet, why haven't we made love in over two months?" she asked unbelievingly.

"I just can't."

"Forget the clothes," she snapped, walking around him to unlock the door.

"Damn it, Bri, just admit it. I'm tired of this!" he yelled.

"Admit what?!" she screamed back at him.

 Trevet took a deep breath. "That Tyrone raped you, or maybe it wasn't rape since you said nothing about it."

Bri stepped to him and looked up directly into his eyes, her eyes darkening with rage. She balled up her hand and punched him in his chest as hard as she could. "I hate you right now,

Trevet!" Turning, she left the room. Bri was at the top of the stairs when she heard his next comment.

"Then he did. Was it as good as he claimed?" he called after her.

Bri rushed back to the bedroom. Trevet was sitting at the foot of the bed. She stood in front of him, and his head rose. She slapped him so hard, her hand stung. "I hate you!" she screamed, tears streaming down her face.

Trevet sat there, holding his face. He knew he deserved that.

"Let me clear something up for you, Trevet. Tyrone didn't rape me. I fought for me and my son's life. And before I go, let me tell you this: I would have killed myself if he had raped me. I would be dead! Do you understand?" She turned and ran down the stairs. Trevet went after her, calling her name.

"What have I done?" Trevet muttered.

"Damn it, where are my keys," she muttered, looking around. Trevet found her in the kitchen, looking through the drawers.

"Brie," Trevet said, his tone desperate.

"No, Trevet."

"Please, Bri, I'm sorry."

Bri turned to him. "You hurt me, Trevet, and you believed a drugged out criminal over me. What does that say to me? It says you don't trust me!"

"Bri, I didn't -- I thought when he said you want..."

Bri put her hands over her ears. "Shut up, Trevet, before I get sick!"

"I just—he …"

"Shut up, Trevet, shut up!" she screamed. "Where are my keys?" she cried, renewing her search.

Trevet held out his hand. There her keys lay in his large hand. She reached for them. He pulled her into his arms.

Bri struggled. "Let me go, Trevet!"

"Bri, I'm sorry. Please. I know I was wrong to feel as I did, but…"

"You didn't trust me. Let me go!" she demanded. "If I did have sex with another man, it would never be Tyrone."

Trevet tensed. "Don't say that, Bri."

"Why not, Trevet? You believed I did it with Tyrone. Let me go!"

"Never! Bri, I love you."

"No, you don't. What's love without trust?"

"You're right. I should have told you how I felt and what Tyrone said."

"Let me go, Trevet," Bri said calmly.

"Are you leaving me?"

Bri shook her head.

He loosened his grip on her but didn't let her go. "I do love you, Bri. You know I do. You are my life." Bri rolled her eyes, turning away.

"You don't believe me?" Trevet questioned, again pulling her in his arms. He lowered his head to kiss her; she turned away.

"Come on, Bri. I've been an ass," he concluded and let her go.

"Yes, you have, Trevet." Bri pushed past him, going up the stairs. She was angry. She truly did hate Trevet at this moment. How could he ever think she would keep something like that from him? Didn't he realize how scared she had been? She would have fought Tyrone to her death before she allowed him to touch her that way again. She went to her studio and locked the door. She needed to be alone. She would sculpt something, and maybe she'd calm down. Right now, she didn't want to see Trevet.

Bri had started a bust of Trevet, that was still wet. She stared at the unfinished piece. Taking the carving tool, she plunged it into the plaster. The pedestal rocked off balance and started to fall. Bri tried to catch it but it fell, and a piece of plaster from the stand stuck into the palm of her hand. Bri looked around the room at the plaster splattered on the floor and walls. She fell to her knees and began to cry.

"Bri!" Trevet called through the door. "Bri!" he said again, trying the door.

"Go away, Trevet," she said hoarsely.

"Bri, are you alright?" Trevet called through the door, turning the knob again.

"Go away, Trevet!"

"Open this door, Bri!"

"Go away, Trevet!"

Bri sat on the floor crying and looking at the gash in her hand, as blood dripped on her lap. She had wet plaster on her shirt, on her face, and in her hair where it had sloshed up on her. She was sitting back on her knees, staring at her hand, and crying when the door crashed open.

Trevet was livid. She didn't acknowledge him; just stared at her hand.

"Never shut me out, Bri!" he yelled at her. She looked up at him, her tears leaving trails through the plaster on her face.

"How does it feel?" She got up and walked past him.

In her bathroom, she tended her hand and ran water for a shower. Trevet didn't follow.

Trevet sat at the kitchen counter. Damn him for being an idiot, she was right. It doesn't feel too good to be shut out, just as he had done to her. Will she ever forgive him? he wondered. She's just angry right now. She had to forgive him, damn it. He had to prove to her that he did trust her and beg her forgiveness.

Trevet stood outside the bedroom. Slowly, he opened the door. The room was shrouded in darkness. Bri stood by the window of the dark room. Trevet walked up behind her, and she stiffened in anticipation of his touch. Trevet closed his eyes, taking in her scent. Her hair was still damp from the shower. She reached up and wiped a strand of hair from her face. He noticed her hand wrapped in a white bandage. "Bri?" he said softly.

"I'm fine," she said and moved away from him.

She then turned to look up at him. "You hurt me, Trevet," she said woefully.

"I know, baby. I'm sorry."

"Don't do it again," she said softly and sat on the side of the bed, her head down. Trevet went to her and kneeled down in front of her. He lifted her head with his finger. She hadn't lowered her head for well over a year; now she was doing it again, all because of him. She looked at him with watery eyes. She loved him so much. Trevet noted the pained looked on her face, because of him.

"Are you going to leave me?" he gently asked.

"I promised I'd never leave you, Trevet," she said softly and lowered her head again. He raised it.

"Do you hate me?"

"No, Trevet. I love you, fool that I am."

His eyes closed for a brief moment of relief. "Bri, I'm sorry. You don't know how sorry I am. My life is nothing without you and Aaron."

"I know, Trevet, I know. I'm nothing without you."

"Could you ever forgive me? I mean, I was foolish," Trevet admitted honestly.

"I've already forgiven you," she said, rubbing his face gently and looking at him intently. She leaned forward and kissed the cheek she had slapped. "I'm sorry I hit you." Her hand then caressed the spot that she had punched. She leaned forward and kissed that spot. "I'm also sorry I punched you."

Trevet reached out and pulled her gown over her head. Watching her intently, he unbuttoned his shirt and stood to remove his pants. Her head followed his movements. She rose before him and pressed her lips to his chest. His arms wrapped around her. He raised her head and kissed her, releasing the pent-up emotions he had for her. She pushed him back and straddled him; allowing him to enter her warm, wet body. His hands touched her breasts, fondling them with gentle hands, as she slowly rode him. Her eyes closed, her head fell back, and she moaned with each motion their bodies made. Trevet rolled her to her back. She looked up at him with passion-glazed eyes, her walls gently squeezing him to fulfillment.

"I love you, Tre. You are all I need," she said, pulling his face to her and kissed him sweetly. Together, they found each other's love and joined, forming a perfect union.

*****

I hope you truly enjoyed Volume 3 from the Found Love Series. The Harrison family journey will continue as they seek love, happiness, and success. Stay tuned and watch as they become a formidable force that will keep you on the edge of your seats. I humbly thank you for being my "sidekicks" on this journey. Again, keep on reading and I will keep on writing.
Vivi

Facebook: Vivian Rose Lee -- Email: vivianroselee22@gmail.com

CPSIA information can be obtained
at www.ICGtesting.com
Printed in the USA
LVHW081507130120
643457LV00018B/2184/P

9 781981 223619